A Lumberjack Christmas
...Revisited

Other PageFree books by Janet Elaine Smith

The Keith Series:
Dunnottar
Marylebone
Par for the Course

Patrick and Grace Mysteries:
In St. Patrick's Custody
Recipe for Murder
Old Habits Die Hard (coming soon)

Women of the Week Series:
Monday Knight
Tuesday Nolan (coming in 2005)

House Call to the Past
A Christmas Dream
My Dear Phebe
Dakota Printer

Copyright © 2004 by Janet Elaine Smith.

All rights reserved. Printed in the United States of America.
No part of this publication may be reproduced, stored in a retrieval system, or transmitted, in any form or by any means electronic, mechanical, photocopying, recording, or otherwise, without the prior written permission of the author.

Cover art by Bonny Crow

ISBN: 1-58961-329-5

Published by PageFree Publishing, Inc.
109 South Farmer Street
Otsego, MI 49078
(269) 692-3926
www.pagefreepublishing.com

A Lumberjack Christmas
...Revisited

By

Janet Elaine Smith

DEDICATION

To Irwin and Jeanne Fershleiser
The only Jewish/Episcopalian Santa
and Mrs. Santa I've ever known.

CONTENTS

Chapter One 9

Chapter Two 14

Chapter Three 19

Chapter Four 25

Chapter Five 30

Chapter Six 36

Chapter Seven 40

Chapter Eight 45

Chapter Nine 50

Chapter Ten 56

Chapter Eleven 62

Chapter Twelve 71

Chapter Thirteen 75

Epilogue 81

...REVISITED 83

Chapter One 85

Chapter Two 89

Chapter Three 92

Chapter Four 95

Chapter Five 99

Chapter Six 102

Chapter Seven 110

Chapter Eight 117

Chapter Nine 121

Chapter Ten 124

Chapter Eleven 132

A Note From The Author 137

CHAPTER ONE

Martha Tinker climbed out of the stagecoach in Hibbing, Minnesota. She looked around, taking in the contents of Main Street. To her right the shingles hanging in front of the various buildings boasted a mercantile, a dressmaker, a physician, and the post office. Glancing to the left she saw a church and a hotel.

Not much of a place, she thought as she picked up her sole suitcase and headed for the hotel.

"I would like a room," she said to the man behind the desk.

"For how long?"

"Just overnight," she replied. "I'm leaving in the morning for Sawbill Landing."

The man's eyes lit up and he gave a full-hearted guffaw.

"What's so amusing?" Martha asked.

"You're going to Sawbill Landing?" His lips twitched as he struggled to contain himself. "Just how are you planning to do that? And *what* do you intend to do once you get there?"

"I expect I'll hire a horse and wagon," she said briskly. "And I'm going to join my fiancé, Max Wilson. Not that it's any of your concern." With a haughty jerk of her chin, Martha pointed her nose toward the kerosene chandelier.

"Ain't no wagons can make it over that trail," the desk clerk said. "And ain't likely nobody's gonna take a little bitsy thing like you out to the likes of Sawbill Landing."

A cold shiver ran up and down Martha's spine. True, it was mid-November and there was already more than a foot of snow on the ground, but this chill came from the inside out.

"Then I'll just have to walk there. Now, are you going to rent me a room for the night?"

"Yes, ma'am," he said, turning the guest ledger toward her and handing her a pen. He read what she wrote and gave her a key. "Upstairs and third door to the right, Miss Tinker."

"And just so you'll know, I'm going to spend several hours in prayer to find a way to get to my destination." She stomped up the steps, ignoring the chortles of the man behind her.

Before she reached the top of the stairs the bell on the door rang, signaling that someone had come in.

Martha turned around just in time to see a tall man dressed in black, standing at the desk. She stopped and listened, strangely drawn to the man.

"Do you have a room available for the night?" he asked, his voice deep and resonant.

"Yes, sir," the desk clerk answered. "How long will you be staying?"

"Just one night, sir. I'm heading for Sawbill Landing come the morning."

Martha nearly toppled down the steps at his response.

At the same time the color drained from the clerk's face. "This is most unusual. Two in one day. I never bought into that prayer business myself," he mumbled, shaking his head.

"Beg your pardon?"

"How do you intend to get there?" the clerk asked the man in black.

"Got myself a horse. Man I got it from said it would make the trip easy. Said he'd done it himself a time or two."

"If you say so." The clerk handed him a pen to sign the guest register.

The newcomer signed, glancing at the preceding entry. "And where is Miss Tinker?"

"Right here," Martha said, making her way back downstairs, her suitcase still clutched in her hand. She extended her hand to shake his and felt a warm tingle as they touched. *You're going to meet Max,* her common sense scolded.

"Pleased to meet you. Dr. Byron Ferguson at your service, ma'am." He felt an immediate attraction to the young lady, so prim and proper in contrast to the women he usually met here in the northern Minnesota woodlands. She didn't look as though she belonged in these parts.

"If you don't mind, sir, I should like to accompany you to Sawbill Landing tomorrow."

"You want to go to Sawbill Landing?" he asked. "But why?"

"My fiancé, Max Wilson, is there. He wrote to me in Boston, asking me to come." She set her suitcase down and took a letter, folded and well-worn, from her handbag and turned it over so only that line showed.

Byron laughed. "I can't believe he'd say that. Are you sure you read all of it?" he asked.

"Of course I did," Martha snapped. "I'm not illiterate! My father saw to it that I was properly educated at the finest schools in Boston!" Her bosom, although not extremely large, seemed to swell to mammoth proportions as she boasted. "He is—*was*—a doctor."

"Well, it seems we have at least one thing in common," Byron said, not acknowledging the change of tense Martha placed her father in. "As I told you when I introduced myself, I'm a doctor, too." He bent over and picked up his black bag, which bore his initials, followed by "MD."

"And what takes you to Sawbill Landing, Doctor Ferguson?"

"This," he said, handing her a telegraph and allowing her to read it in its entirety.

> *Need help immediately—*
> *Stop*
> *Men dying faster than flies—*
> *Stop*
> *Come or send someone—*
> *Stop!*

Martha went weak in the knees, and her face cooled as the blood drained from it. *What if it meant Max?* What would she do if he were among the fatalities? *No!* He had to be all right. Surely he would have let her know if—but that was pure foolishness! How could he let her know if he had? No, she would not even entertain the thought.

"Are you okay?" Dr. Ferguson asked. "Here, let me help you over to the sofa so you can sit down."

Her purse, which she'd been clutching tightly, dropped to the floor with a loud *thud*.

"I'll be…"

And she landed right smack dab in his arms.

Byron carried her to the sofa, where he laid her down, and then raced back to get his medical bag. He pulled out a vial of smelling salts and waved them under her nose until she responded.

"I'm sorry." Martha sat up, grabbing her head to stop the room from twirling around. "I don't mean to be a bother."

"I don't think it's a good idea for you to go out to the logging camp," Byron said. "There's no telling what I might find once I get there. If and when whatever it is that has hit the camp lets go of the place I'll send for you." He paused. "Better yet, I'll come back and get you myself."

"No," Martha argued. "I have to go to Max. I have to see that he's alive and well." Her eyes filled with tears. "If anything happened to him—he's all I have left."

"Your parents?" Byron asked.

"Dead." She lowered her head. "They died in a fire. I was away at finishing school or I'd have been with them. So, don't you see? I have to get to Max. I don't have anybody else in the world. I have to go!"

"I still don't think it's a good idea," Byron said.

The desk clerk stood in the background nodding his head in agreement. "I promise I'll come back for you as soon as it is safe."

Martha remained undaunted. "I can be of great use to you," she insisted. "I often helped my father in his practice. I'm not a nurse, but I know as much as many of them. Perhaps more. If it is as bad as it sounds, it will be too much for you to handle alone."

"I told you no," Byron said, sticking to his guns.

"Sounds to me like she could be real helpful."

He was surprised when the desk clerk stuck his two cents in.

"I guess a man can tell when he's licked," Byron said. "Okay, little lady. We'll leave as soon as it's daylight. But if it gets too rough for you on the trip you have to agree that you'll let me bring you back here."

"That's fair," Martha said. She'd freeze to death before she'd give in. She had to get to Sawbill Landing. She had to get to Max!

"You better go on up and get a good night's sleep," Byron suggested.

"You want something to eat first?" the desk clerk asked them both. "The Missus dishes up a mighty fine stew for the evening meal. I can get her to serve you a little early, if you'd like."

"That would be fine," Byron said, picking up Martha's suitcase and starting up the steps. "Which room?"

"Third one on the right," the desk clerk answered. "Right across the hall from yours."

Byron found relief in knowing she would be close to him. He wanted to keep an eye on her, although he didn't have any idea why.

Martha, on the other hand, bristled at this arrangement. "I don't need a guard dog."

"Only two rooms I've got empty," the clerk said simply. "I didn't plan it that way. Just like nobody planned two people showing up within minutes of each other, both headed for Sawbill Landing."

Martha shrugged her shoulders. "And I hadn't even prayed about it yet," she said. "An answer to prayer before it was even uttered."

Byron laughed. "I've been called a lot of things in my life, but even as a doctor I don't know that anybody has ever considered me an answer to a prayer. Yes, little lady, I have a feeling there might be a whole lot of *firsts* where you're concerned."

* * *

The desk clerk had been right. Maybe it was because she was ravenous, but the venison stew his wife served them was the best thing she had eaten in days. Maybe weeks. Probably since the last meal she had shared with her mother and father before she left for finishing school. Byron also appeared to enjoy it immensely. In fact, he ate with such gusto that he did not, much to Martha's relief, indulge in any conversation. Before he could empty his mouth, Martha thanked the hotel owners, excused herself and went up to her room, where her suitcase—and the most glorious feather bed she had ever seen—awaited her.

CHAPTER TWO

It seemed like an eternity had passed since that fateful day when she'd learned of her parents' death. Now, as she reflected on all that had happened since then, she was surprised that it had been only four months.

Stunned by the loss of her family and her home, she had been at a complete loss when she saw the ad.

> *Wanted: Future bride for lonely man in northern Minnesota logging camp.*

It was her way of escape. Her salvation. She knew what she had to do. After answering the ad, she'd wondered if she'd lost her mind. But she poured her heart out to Max. And then his reply came.

They had exchanged only two letters, but when he said he wanted her to come, she blocked the "someday." That's why it had bothered her so much when the doctor had questioned whether she'd read all of Max's letter. She should never have shown it to him.

Her tears flowed freely. It was the first time she had allowed herself that luxury. Oh how she wished the pillow could absorb her fears and heartaches like it swallowed her tears. What if Max had died from whatever epidemic had attacked the camp? What if she was all alone again? What if she and Dr. Ferguson never made it through the snow to Sawbill Landing?

Frightful ideas danced like the moonbeams that filtered through the lace curtains and created cobweb-like images on the ceiling.

What if she never even got to see Max? She'd formed a mental picture of him from the way he had described himself in his letter. *So tender*, she thought, as she ran the memorized lines through her mind. He'd copied the verses he sent from famous poets, but what kind of a man knew and cared about such things as poetry if he wasn't a true romantic at heart?

Her mind wandered to her father. He'd often whispered sweet nothings to her mother, and Martha still remembered her mother's voice, cooing contentedly. How she missed them!

Finally, lost in a world far from her own, she drifted off to sleep. Her last conscious thought was that she wasn't sure she wanted to wake up in the morning.

* * *

She awoke with a start and sat up in bed. She tossed the covers off, then pulled them back up as the cold slapped her in the face. She rubbed her eyes and looked out the window. It was still dark, and she was tempted to lie down and try to get back to sleep, but then she heard the door across the hallway creak.

Wrapping the quilt around her, she scampered to the door to see where Dr. Ferguson was going in the middle of the night.

"Good morning," she said, trying to sound cheerful when she saw him tiptoeing down the hall.

"What are you doing up so early?" He pulled his black hat down over his forehead, nearly hiding his eyes.

"I—I didn't want to miss my ride," she said, pulling the quilt tighter around herself. "If you'll just wait a few minutes, I'll be right down." As she started to go back into her room, she caught her toe on the corner of the quilt and went sprawling in a most unladylike manner—right at the good doctor's feet.

"Oh, my!" she exclaimed, her face warming with embarrassment. "I...I didn't mean for that to happen."

Dr. Ferguson burst out laughing. She couldn't tell if it was from her appearance as a huge jumble in the middle of the hallway or from her prim and proper reaction to the fall.

"It's not funny," Martha scolded "Some doctor you are! I could be hurt!"

"Allow me to examine you," he said, leaning over her.

She clutched the quilt tighter to her body and tried to sound dignified. "I'm quite sure I will be all right. But you could assist me in getting to my feet."

Dr. Ferguson extended a hand, but as she reached for the quilt, it slipped. Squealing, she tugged at the quilt, tucked it around her neck, then struggled to her feet on her own power.

"That was a most remarkable recovery," he said, his eyes dancing with merriment. "I must remember to get your recipe. Surely such a remedy will come in handy in my practice."

Martha hurried into her room, slamming the door behind her and slipping the chain across it. A woman couldn't be too careful, even with a doctor, she thought as she dashed to the chair and grabbed her clothing. There was no time to worry about getting clean garb from her suitcase. He was just infuriating enough to ride off without her. And if there was only one thing she knew, it was that she had to get to Sawbill Landing—to Max.

* * *

Her suitcase seemed much heavier as she pulled it down the stairs with her. She wondered how she would manage to carry it with them on the horses. Perhaps the desk clerk could offer a suggestion. She certainly wasn't about to ask the doctor for his help. She'd seen more than enough of his able assistance.

Reaching the hotel lobby, she found the clerk's wife waiting for her. "I have breakfast prepared," she said, smiling warmly. "Come with me.

"I don't have time," Martha protested. "I have to get to Sawbill Landing with Dr. Ferguson. My fiancé…"

"Don't worry, the doctor is having breakfast, too. And as for your fiancé… I know, I know. John told me all about it. Young love. Oofta! I've long ago forgotten it."

"Too bad," Martha said, offering her condolences. She didn't intend to explain that love had nothing to do with her present situation. Salvation, perhaps, from her problems, but love? Hardly. Martha knew she was not in love with Max Wilson. She didn't even know if she was *in like* with the man. In fact, she didn't even know the man!

Thoughts tumbled around in her head like pebbles in the river. Why on earth had she ever thought this was a good idea? Boston boasted a number of eligible bachelors, many of whom had tried to pursue her. None of them, however, could offer the thrill of adventure or the challenge of facing the unknown. Not the way Max Wilson could. And his letter was most persuasive.

"Thought you were never going to get up," John Anderson said as Martha and Helga joined him and Dr. Ferguson in the dining room.

Martha looked at the black mantle clock, surprised to see that it was almost eight o'clock. "It's still dark out."

"Of course," John said. "It's almost December."

Martha realized how far north she was and remembered the stories of the midnight sun. So this was what it was like?

"How was your journey so far?" John asked.

"The train ride went quite well," Martha said, "but when we got into the stage coach it was quite uncomfortable."

"Uncomfortable?" Dr. Ferguson asked. "If it was anything like the trip I had, it was downright miserable! I couldn't sleep a wink the whole way!"

"You thought you might sleep on the stage?" Martha asked, laughing. "But surely you have ridden on it before."

"Once or twice," the doctor replied. "Although I usually prefer to go on horseback. Always did, before I lost poor Nellie." He bowed his head and took his black felt hat from his knee, where he normally propped it while at the table, placing it over his heart. "May you rest in peace," he said softly.

Martha had often heard about the *cowboys* out west who were closer to their horses than they were to their mothers, but somehow Dr. Ferguson didn't look at all the way she had pictured a cowboy. She'd read about the thrilling lives they led, and had even seen a few pictures in the papers back home. No, none of them looked at all like Dr. Ferguson. They wore dungarees and boots, while he was clad in a black suit and white shirt. He looked quite professional, considering that he was about to head into the wilds.

"I'm ready whenever you are," Martha said, sipping the hot coffee, her little finger poised delicately like she had learned to do in finishing school.

"You should wait here until I see how dangerous it is," Dr. Ferguson repeated. He shook his finger at her. "And I mean it! It isn't a good idea for you to go. I never should have let you talk me into taking you along."

"And I told you I can be of great help to you," she said, just as dogmatically. "I'm going, and that's that."

"Better get another horse from Sam," John Anderson said. "Can't get there with just one. Not and haul her suitcase."

"Then we'll have to leave your things behind," Dr. Ferguson said. "It will be easier with just one animal to tend to. Pretty hard on them, this kind of weather and all."

"One horse?" Martha asked. "But there are two of us."

"That's right," Dr. Ferguson said, grinning. "Got a problem with that?"

"Um, no, sir," Martha said. She knew she would do whatever it took to get to Sawbill Landing and Max, no matter what that entailed. She shrugged her shoulders in defeat. "But there are a few things I will need. I'll take my valise back upstairs and take them out." She turned to Helga. "Do you have a small bag I might borrow?"

"Of course, child," Helga answered. "And you just leave your other belongings up in the room. We'll put them in the attic until you can get them. We'll see that they are safe, won't we, John?"

Martha grinned. It appeared that Helga had the upper hand in this family. She couldn't imagine John arguing with her about anything—not after she gave him one of *those* looks.

Martha hurried upstairs, once again dragging the suitcase with her. She couldn't explain it, but it seemed to get heavier each time she had to move it. It wouldn't be fair to a horse to have to lug all of this along.

Enough of this nonsense, she warned herself. She had to stay strong, for the trip and for whatever awaited them once they got to Sawbill Landing. This was no time to chicken out on anything. She had no alternative; an unknown fiancé was better than no one at all. And without Max that was exactly what she had: no one.

She hurried to sort through her belongings, collected the bare necessities, and shoved them into the small leather pouch Helga had given her. "Well, Dr. Byron Ferguson, I do hope that isn't too much for your precious horse to carry!"

Martha went to the window and peered at the street below. It looked so calm and peaceful. She took in every detail, trying to preserve it in her memory. She wondered how long it would be before she saw the streets of Hibbing again.

She jumped at the intrusion of Dr. Ferguson into the picture. She knew she shouldn't have trusted him. He was leaving for Sawbill Landing—without her!

Martha grabbed the bag and sped down the steps, her skirts hiked high above her ankles, and raced out the door.

"Oh, no you don't!" she yelled at him, causing several passersby to turn and stare. "You aren't getting out of here without me!"

"Didn't intend to," he said, laughing. "Spunk! That's what my mother used to call it. Well, Miss Martha Tinker, it appears that you've got more than your share of it. I was just hooking on the blankets so we'd be ready to go." In a sudden moment of compassion he said, "Mrs. Anderson gave me two quilts for you. Said she doubted you had any in that suitcase of yours."

"She's right," Martha said. "Guess I just figured Max would have plenty of bedclothes. I didn't think..."

"Typical female!" Dr. Ferguson grumbled. "They never think!"

Martha handed him the pouch, which he fastened on with a rope. Then, taking her by surprise, he pulled her into his arms and lifted her onto the horse. Before he knew what hit him, his face burned from the slap of her open palm.

"You have a better way to get up there?" he asked, rubbing his cheek.

"Let's go!" she said, not bothering to apologize. She didn't know what she had expected, but it wasn't the feeling she got from being in his arms.

CHAPTER THREE

They rode through the streets. The people who smiled as they passed left Martha extremely conscious of how close they had to sit to each other, her back rubbing against the warmth of his chest, even in the cold. "Nice couple," one woman remarked to another. "Wonder who they are?"

"Suppose it's the new preacher and his wife?" the other one speculated.

"Good day," Byron said, tipping his hat and smiling without denying or acknowledging the assumption.

Martha jabbed him in the stomach with her elbow. "Why didn't you tell them who we are?" she asked.

"And spoil their fun?" Byron retorted. "Where's your sense of humor?"

"Guess I left it in Boston," she said. "I don't see anything particularly amusing."

"Funny," Byron said.

"What's funny?" Martha asked.

"Funny," Byron repeated. "You're in Minnesota now, not Boston. In Boston, perhaps things are *amusing*. In Minnesota they are *funny.*"

"Well, excuse me!" Martha said. "I didn't realize you were an expert on languages."

"It appears there's a lot about me that you don't know, and vice versa," Byron said. "Maybe we should make it a game on our trip to Sawbill Landing to learn as much as we can about each other."

Martha squirmed uncomfortably. "I think you already know too much about me," she said. "And I have no real interest in knowing anything more about you, Dr. Ferguson. I know more than I care to already."

"Well!" he said, puffing so the steam from his mouth nearly blinded her for a few seconds. "If we're going to be in close company for the entire trip, don't you think you could call me Byron? Dr. Ferguson seems so formal."

"Dr. Ferguson will do just fine," Martha said. "We are close now because we have to be, but once we get to Sawbill Landing, well, that will be different."

"I thought you said you were going to help me treat the men who have been stricken out there," he reminded her. "That might be a bit hard to do if we aren't even on speaking terms."

Martha knew he had her there. The only reason he had allowed her to go with him was so she could—and *would*—help him. This was no time to back out on that offer. She wouldn't put it past him to dump her in a snow bank and leave her for some stranger to find; how long that might take was anybody's guess.

"All right," she said reluctantly. "Byron it is, but that's not to say I like it."

"You don't like the name Byron?" he asked, teasing her. She suspected his eyes were twinkling, even though she couldn't see them with him sitting behind her.

"Nothing wrong with the name," she said. *It's the man who creates the problem.* A spark of something akin to longing ignited and coursed through her body as he adjusted himself behind her; she felt him even closer than he had been before, if that was possible.

"Glad that's settled," he said, jabbing at the horse with his boots to make him run faster.

"What's your hurry?" Martha asked. "Isn't that hard on the horse?"

"Not as hard as it will be if we take too long," he said. "There's a storm brewing."

Martha chortled. "That's ridiculous!" she said. "There isn't a sound anywhere. Listen, you can't even hear a bird."

"That's the point," Byron said. "It's never this still in the woods unless there's trouble brewing. The birds and the animals, they can sense it. They've all gone for shelter."

"And you know this because...?" Martha asked, shaking her head in denial at his ability as a seer.

"I've lived here long enough to have learned the ways of the forest," he explained. "We have about three hours to ride before we get to the camp. Let's just hope we can outrun it."

"I'll believe it when I see it," Martha said, looking upwards. "It's as clear a sky as I've ever seen."

"Look over there," Byron said, pointing to the north. "It's starting already."

There, way off in the distance, hung a tiny black cloud. It didn't look big enough to do any damage, but she had to admit that it did appear somewhat threatening, in spite of its size. She wanted to spur the horse even more, just in case.

"Tell me about your father's medical practice," Byron said, glad for the common ground they could share as they rode.

"Not much to tell. He had his regular run of normal cases: delivering babies, typhoid fever, ague, measles, rheumatism, heart palpitations, the usual."

"Who were his patients?" he asked, intrigued by how nonchalant she could make the matter of life and death appear.

"Just regular people," Martha said.

"Poor people? Rich people? Old people? Young people? And which did he like best?"

Martha smiled at his implication. So he thought she came from a family of stuck up snobs, did he? Well, she'd set him straight in a hurry.

"He saw many of the elite of the town, it's true," she said. She straightened up to her fullest height. "But he was at his best when he went down to the docks and helped the men coming off the ships."

She stopped, and Byron waited, suddenly seeing a new side to his companion. Maybe she could be of some use at the logging camp after all. He tried to picture her down on the docks, helping her father examine men who were probably filthy after long weeks—perhaps even months—at sea. And from all he had heard about sailors, their mouths were probably even more foul than their bodies.

After a long silence he asked, "Did you help him on the docks, too? Or just in his office?"

After hesitating, she finally said, a new warmth in her voice, "I loved working with the men down there." She felt the color rise in her cheeks again. "I mean, I liked feeling helpful. Useful. None of the other doctors would treat them. Often they couldn't pay. Other times they would pay with treasures they'd found on their journeys." Martha paused. "Mother and Father had so many of them in their home. Each one had a special story." She swallowed hard, barely able to continue speaking. "Now they're all gone."

Byron felt her body quiver against him as she sobbed softly. He freed one hand from the reins and tenderly rubbed her shoulder and arm.

"It feels good, doesn't it?" he asked.

She wriggled, trying to escape his touch. *Yes*, she admitted to herself, *it feels far too good*.

"What?" Martha asked, squirming uncomfortably.

"Helping the less fortunate, of course," Byron replied, smiling.

"Yes," she said, quick to agree with him. "On Wednesdays we—Father and I—would go and visit the wives and children of the sailors who lived near the docks. They lived in such squalor! Sometimes we tried to give them things, but they were proud, even in the little they had. But then we discovered that if we gave them food and told them it was for the children, the mothers always accepted it gratefully."

Byron longed to tighten his grip around her, to hold onto her vulnerability. It must have been very difficult for her to decide to leave the only home she'd ever known for a strange, forsaken land, as foreign to her as if she had sailed to far-off Australia. Hoping to ease her tension, at least a little, he changed the subject.

"Tell me about Max Wilson," he said, expecting to invoke a smile from her at the one known factor she traveled towards.

Instead of relief, he sensed even more tension than before. He wished he could recant his question.

"What do you want to know?" she finally asked.

"Well," Byron said, "for starters, how long have you known him?"

"Not long."

"Is he from Boston, too?"

"No," Martha said. She shook her head, surprising herself at how little she knew about the man she was going to marry in a matter of days. "I mean, um, I don't know."

Byron debated about whether to pursue this line of questioning, or if he should drop this and discuss the weather. No, he decided, they had already tried that and they couldn't even agree on that. *Charge ahead.*

"Where did you meet him?" he asked.

"I—I haven't met him," Martha answered. "That is, not in person." She paused, then added, "But we have written, and he writes wonderful letters!" Another pause. "He is *quite* romantic!"

"How so?" Byron asked.

"He writes beautiful poetry in almost every letter," Martha explained. "He—he must love me. He couldn't write such lovely things if he didn't."

Byron shook his head, glad she was in front of him. There was something wrong here. She obviously had no idea what she was getting herself into. He didn't want to see her get hurt—either physically or emotionally. Suddenly, he knew what he had to do; it was up to him to protect her—from all the men at Sawbill Landing—perhaps even from Max Wilson.

First thing he would do when they arrived at the camp, he decided, was to find Max Wilson before she found him. He would question the man to see if his feelings for her were genuine; if they weren't, he would give him a stern warning.

"How did you decide to marry him?" Byron asked. "Did he ask you in one of his letters?"

Martha's back bristled like a cat ready to pounce on an innocent mouse. "Of course he asked me!" she shouted at him. "What kind of a woman do you think I am?"

Suddenly it struck her; Max had not really asked her to marry him at all. She had just assumed, from the things he said, things like, *I dream at night that you are here with me*, and *I wish you could come…sometime.* But no, if she was absolutely honest with herself, he had never asked for her hand in marriage. Not in so many words. Was she making a complete fool of herself, traveling halfway across the country to a man who probably didn't even want to see her?

"Well, if you need me," Byron offered tenderly, "I'm available."

"I can take care of myself," Martha said with determination. *I hope.* She made a silent prayer that God would help her prove that statement true. "I don't want to discuss this anymore," she said, tossing her head for emphasis.

Byron was not easily dismissed. "Do you love him?"

"Love! What do you know about love? And why does marriage always have to be about love? Besides, this is none of your business!"

"You're right," Byron said, "but I have a feeling that your mother and father would appreciate someone looking out for you."

"My mother and father can't appreciate anything!" Martha sputtered angrily. "I told you, they're both dead!"

"And whose fault is that?" Byron asked, sensing her anger.

"No one's," she said. "I don't blame anyone." *Or do I?* she wondered. She hadn't found anybody to blame. God was handy. Why not blame Him?

"It's a good thing we're almost there. The storm is getting closer." He no sooner spoke than huge fluffy white snowflakes began to fall.

Martha shook her head again, surprised at how nervous he was. "This is beautiful!" she exclaimed. "It's not a storm!"

"Trust me, it's coming."

Martha was relieved that at least the predicted storm had brought about a change of topic, since he'd ignored her request to drop the subject of her engagement to Max.

They rode in silence for some time. In a flash, the wind began to howl and the snow began to whirl about them, nearly hiding the trail they had been following. Martha was filled with fear. Maybe they would get lost and die out here in the wilderness. Would anybody ever find them?

"There it is!" Byron shouted, pointing to the collection of tarpaper shacks just ahead of them.

He urged the horse to move faster. When they pulled in to camp he jumped down, helping Martha off before running between the rows of shacks, yelling "Doctor in camp! Doctor in camp!"

Men emerged from the shacks, some hale and hearty and others stumbling, apparently victims of the epidemic he had been warned about.

Martha grabbed hold of the first man she saw and said "Max Wilson! I have to find Max Wilson! Where is he?"

"In the long house with the others," the man replied, pointing to a big log building.

Martha ran toward the long house, lifting her skirts slightly and nearly tripping on the snow, which was already quite deep. She pushed the heavy door open and went inside.

Byron, seeing her running, followed her and entered the long house just in time to see her drop to her knees at the sight. There, in the log building, were rows and rows of corpses. Max Wilson was dead!

CHAPTER FOUR

When she regained consciousness, Byron was kneeling over her, waving the smelling salts under her nose.

"What happened?" she asked. "Where am I?"

"You—*we*—are at Sawbill Landing. Don't you remember our ride out here?"

Martha rubbed her head, and little by little things came into focus in her mind.

"Max?" she asked, closing her eyes, hoping that would make the bodies she had seen disappear.

"I'm sorry," Byron said, stashing the bottle back into his medical bag and taking her hand in his. "Maybe if I'd been here sooner."

"Don't blame yourself. You came as soon as you got word."

"I did." Byron gazed at the bodies. He shuddered, remembering the fields of men he had seen in similar rows when he served in the Civil War, just four short years ago. He'd struggled to push images such as these into the back of his mind. He couldn't help but wonder if tragedy and mortality followed him.

"Go get Maya," said one of the men who had followed them into the long house. One of the lumberjacks hurried away.

Byron looked down at Martha, wishing he could make everything all right for her, but knowing her hurt would go far deeper before it lessened. Trying to lighten the moment, he teased, "I thought you were going to help me. I don't see how that's possible with you lying here flat on your back."

"I'm sorry," she said, "but can't you see that I am in mourning?" Her head screamed at her: *How can you be in mourning over losing something you never had and someone you never even knew?*

To Martha's great relief, a woman ran into the longhouse. She was clad in a pair of wool trousers just like all the men were wearing and had an exact replica of their red and black buffalo-checked wool shirt. Martha smiled, despite the way she felt, when she saw a tiny ruffle of white peeking out at the neck and the wrists.

"I'm Maya Koski," the woman said, pushing the doctor aside to get down beside Martha. "I'll take over here. You go see to the others. There are scads of men who are *really* sick."

"I didn't mean to take him away from the ones who need him," Martha said, turning to Byron. "She's right. You go do what you can to help them." She swallowed hard as she added, "Maybe you can keep them alive."

"Unlike Max." He strode away, his steps long but heavy. "I'll be back when I can."

"Can you sit up now?" Maya asked Martha.

"I think so." She had never been a sissy before and she didn't expect to start now. Certainly not with so much to do. And she had promised to help Byron as he examined the lumberjacks.

She sat up slowly, then got to her feet, glad to find that the floor steady beneath her.

"I have to go help Byron," she insisted, hardly realizing she had called him by his first name, as he had asked. "He needs me."

"Is Byron your husband?" Maya asked.

Martha was embarrassed by the question, wondering how Maya could have been so misled.

"No," she said, giggling at the idea. "We just met yesterday."

"Then what are you doing at Sawbill Landing?" Maya asked. "And how do you know—um—I'm not quite sure who that was."

"You don't know?" Martha asked. "He is the doctor they sent for. And I am—*was*— here to marry Max. He asked me to come to him. I didn't have anyone else, so it just seemed like the right thing to do."

"I'm so sorry," Maya said. She clapped her hand over her mouth. "Oh, dear, you did know, didn't you?"

"That Max is…dead?" Martha asked. "I do now, or at least I assumed he was. They told me I'd find him here—but these men are all dead."

"We'll have to find a way to get you back to Hibbing so you can go home. I'll ask the men."

"No!" Martha nearly shouted. "I don't want to go…*home!* I don't have a home." She gave Maya the shortened version of the fire and her parents' death. "So you see, I guess I am home."

Maya's face brightened. "You mean you might stay here?" She wrapped Martha in her arms like she would a daughter. "Oh, thank the good Lord!"

Martha's mouth formed a smile, even though salty tears continued trickling down her cheeks. She liked this woman.

"You see," Maya explained, "I am the only woman in camp. I do the cooking and the laundry. It would be so nice to have another woman around."

Martha ducked her head. "I've never done anyone's laundry before," she admitted, "and I'm a terrible cook. The men would probably all get sick if I fed them."

Maya laughed. "Your mother did everything for you all your life?" she asked.

"Oh, no," Martha said. "We had servants."

"You're a southerner?" Maya asked.

"No," Martha said, laughing with her. "I'm from Boston. I said *servants*, not *slaves*. There's a big difference. We treated them like they were part of the family, and Father paid them very well. So what good am I going to be here? I'll probably just be in your way. All I've ever done is study music on the pianoforte and go to finishing school."

Maya looked puzzled. "You finished school? That's good, no?"

"Not *finished* school," Martha said. "*Finishing* school."

"Well, it looks to me like you are finished with it now. There is no school here."

Martha laughed again. "You said you came from Finland? Maybe what we need here is a *Finnish* school."

The two women were nearly in hysterics when Byron came back inside. *It must be a case of nervous release*, he reasoned. He would ask Martha about it, but not right now.

"If you can control yourself," he said to Martha, "I could sure use your help. A lot of the men are burning up; I could use you to apply some cold compresses."

"I'm sorry," Martha said, wiping the tears from her eyes. "I didn't mean to make light of the situation. It's just…"

"Go on," Maya said. "I'll go tend to the cooking. Before long it will be time for the evening meal. Even if they are sick, ach, they eat like a bunch of wild boars."

"I've got a cluster of cots set up in the meeting house," Byron said as he and Martha plowed their way through the snow. "There's a good warm fire in there, and we can keep the infected men away from the others to try and prevent it from spreading."

* * *

Byron and Martha worked together in perfect unison. He marveled at her ability to react; it was as though she could sense what he needed before he asked for it.

Fevers began to break, whether from the combination of medicines he gave them or the cold rags Martha applied, he didn't know. But soon some of the men began to rally and many even began sitting up.

"I think I can handle it now," Byron said, looking outside and seeing that the sun had already set. "Why don't you go over and get yourself something to eat?"

"I'm okay," she said. "I would rather stay here." She felt strangely safe in his presence. Maybe it was because he was the only person she knew. Him and Maya.

"I can't have you dropping off because of starvation. You haven't had anything to eat since this morning when we left the hotel in Hibbing."

"Neither have you," she reminded him. "Tell you what, I'll go find Maya and see if I can get something for both of us to eat. I'll bring it back here and we can eat it together."

"Why, Miss Tinker! Are you asking me to dine with you?"

She blushed. "No. Well, yes, I guess I am." She felt like her tongue was about to trip over her feet. "But I didn't mean…" She turned away from him so he couldn't look at her. "I'll be back in just a minute."

"I'm counting," Byron joked, pulling out his shiny gold pocket watch, popping open its lid, and not taking his eyes off it.

Martha hurried out of the meeting house to look for Maya. She met one of the lumberjacks and stopped dead in her tracks. She tipped her head up as far as it would go and still wasn't sure she had seen the top of his head. She had never seen such a man in her life. She had heard of giants, of course, but she always thought them purely mythological creatures. This man could make a believer out of her in a hurry.

"You lost, little lady?" he asked, his voice booming to match his size.

Martha shivered. She didn't know if she should tell him what she was looking for or turn around and run. Contemplating the situation, she decided there was no way she could outrun him, so she might as well ask him what she needed to know.

"Could you tell me where to find Maya Koski?" Martha asked. She could barely hear her own voice, and she wasn't at all sure it would reach up to his ears. Fortunately, he seemed to understand what she wanted.

"Third shack on the right," he said. He put his hand out towards Martha and she was afraid he was going to pick her up and have her for his own lunch. "Hjelmer Finseth," he said. "And your name?"

"M-M-Martha Tinker," she stammered. "Thank you, sir." And then she did run, as fast as her legs would carry her, past the first shack, then the second shack and on to the third shack. She pushed the door open and barged inside, landing on the closest bench and nearly collapsing.

"Are you all right?" Maya asked, hurrying to her side.

"Yes," Martha said, panting for breath. "I just saw the biggest man I've ever seen!"

The men sitting on the benches with tin plates in front of them began to laugh. "Must be Hjelmer!" one of them said.

"Yes," Martha said. "That's what he said." She took a deep breath and asked, "Who is he? Or *what*?"

"He's the man who started Sawbill Landing," one of the men explained. "If it wasn't for Hjelmer, we'd probably all be dead. Or at least without good jobs like we have here."

Martha listened, enrapt with the tale as it began to unfold.

"He sent letters to Minneapolis to tell us about the great forests here. He said people all over America needed wood. Wood for lumber, wood for houses, wood for furniture, even wood for making paper!"

Another man picked the story up. "He had enough money to pay us all until we sold the wood in the spring. He set up the sawmill. It's the only one like it in these parts. He said he built it *yust like da vuns back home in Sveden, yeah, sure, ya betcha!*"

They all roared at the imitation of Hjelmer's accent. Finally one of the men looked at Martha and said, "I don't know what it is about you, little lady, but you're good for us. You know, I think that's the first time any of us have laughed in over a week."

Martha fidgeted with the scarf wrapped around her neck. She wasn't sure if she should be flattered or in fear for her life. These men were anything but trustworthy, by the looks of them. Still, she sensed the camaraderie. If she could provide some amusement for them, even at her own expense, then so be it. Maybe she could be useful at the logging camp. Even without Max.

CHAPTER FIVE

Martha walked into the meeting hall laden with a pile of food large enough to feed the whole logging camp.

"Maya says she will be along shortly with food for the sick men," she said.

"And that is...?" Byron asked.

"Food for us."

"Us? As in *you and me* us?" His eyes bulged at the sight of the food as he lifted the towel covering it and peeked to see what it contained. "Mmm!" he said as the aroma of the fare wafted into the open air. "I didn't realize how hungry I was."

"Hungry enough to eat all of this?" Martha asked. "Except, of course, what I devour first. You were right; I am hungry too." She grabbed a piece of homemade sourdough bread and dipped it into the bowl of venison stew. Lifting it to her mouth, she savored it for a long time before she finally swallowed.

"Maya be praised!" Byron said as he too took a bite. "And God, too!"

Martha stopped chewing and set her slice of bread down.

"Is there something wrong with it?" Byron asked, suddenly hit by the idea that perhaps what the men in camp were suffering from was as simple as something they had eaten.

"No," Martha said, bowing her head and sitting silently. After a few moments she looked up and continued eating.

Byron watched her with interest. He assumed she had paused to say grace. He shifted in his seat and followed suit. He had not said a "thank you" to God for a meal—or anything else, for that matter—in more years than he could remember. *Some things*, he thought, *you just take for granted. Like life in general.* As he looked around him at the men groaning in pain, he realized that he had a great deal to be thankful for. He vowed to do better in that department.

He glanced over at Martha, busily chewing away on her food, and thought that of all things to be grateful for, she should head the list. She had indeed been a lot of help with the men. When things settled down he would have to remember to tell her how much he appreciated her.

Maya came with the food for the men, as she had promised. She had recruited several of the still-healthy men to help her carry it.

Byron went over to look at it. "Is it the same as we had?" he asked Maya.

"Yes," she said. "But I ran out of mushrooms, so it isn't as good as what we had the other day."

"Mushrooms?" Byron's tone was urgent. "You fed the men mushrooms?"

"Sure," Maya said. "That's what made it so special. The men who came in first said it was so good they ate all of it up before the second shift came in. I had to make up a fresh batch, but I didn't have any more mushrooms."

"Take a look at the men here who are sick," Byron instructed Maya. "Were any of them in the second shift, or were they all in the first group?"

Maya looked at the men, studying each one carefully.

"I'm not sure," she said, scratching her head and walking among the cots to see who was there.

"I, um, I think they were all in the first group. Or at least most of them were." She continued making the rounds of the men, trying to remember. "Yes, I am sure they were all in the first group. Why?"

"Do you have any more of the mushrooms left at all? Even one?"

"I don't know," she said, her voice hesitant. Finally, she asked the inevitable question she didn't really want answered. "I didn't do this, did I?"

"Of course not," Byron said, putting his hands on her shoulders to give her strength. "Even if the mushrooms were bad, you couldn't have known."

"Back in the home country, we never worried about the mushrooms. They were always good. I didn't know they could spoil."

"They probably didn't spoil," Byron said. "But some of the mushrooms that grow wild here are poisonous."

"No!" Maya cried. "It can't be! I would never feed the men anything poison! Why, even Uno died! I would never kill my Uno! Never!"

"Of course you wouldn't," Byron said. "Come on, let's go see if we can find a mushroom."

As they started to leave, Martha said, "Don't worry about the men. I'll stay and watch them. If anything happens that I can't handle, I'll send somebody for you."

"All right," Byron said. "But be careful. We don't know for sure that's what it was. It could still be something contagious." He went back to her and pulled her scarf up over her mouth. "Keep that on," he said. "I don't want to lose you."

A warm tingle ran through Martha. He didn't want to lose her! Like she had lost Max. Like Maya had lost Uno. Like so many others had lost their own lives. She couldn't risk losing Byron, either. She knew she had no right to make that claim on him. But, he had said it first.

* * *

Martha sat on the edge of a vacant cot. Just a few hours ago, when they first arrived at the camp, a man had occupied it; now he was in the long house with the other men who had not survived.

She tugged at the leather pack which held all the belongings she had been allowed to bring with her. Taking out her Bible, she began to read, but the words blurred as tears ran down her face. Life was not fair! She had lost her parents, her home, and now the man she hoped would give her a way of escape from her loneliness.

She tried to pray, but the words of her heart bounced back at her from the pitch-covered roof on the meeting hall. God seemed almost as far away as everyone else in her life.

She was not sure how much time had passed when Byron finally came back. His face looked troubled.

"Bad news?"

"It was the mushrooms," he said. "At least now we know what it is and that it isn't contagious." He reached over and pulled the scarf from her face. She didn't understand why, but his gesture made her smile.

"That looks much better," he said, returning the smile. He studied her like he might a puzzling case. "This hasn't been easy for you, has it?"

"No," she said, the tears still flowing freely. "I don't know what to do. Or why this has all happened." She raised her voice slightly as she asked, "Where is God in all this?"

Byron winced. This was no time for her to get fanatical on him. He had been brought up in the church. He had even received awards for never missing Sunday school. But that was a long time ago. Once he began to study medicine, he began to question everything he had learned as a child. Then when he got to the war, things just got worse. He couldn't begin to understand why God would allow so much suffering. He wasn't even sure now that there was a God.

He wondered why she made him feel so uneasy, recalling his faith of his earlier years. Why would she turn to God with all this sickness and death around her?

Suddenly he realized that while she had made him feel guilty by her simple motion of saying a table grace, she had not spoken a word about whether or not he should trust in God. He smiled again and breathed a sigh of relief. She was definitely a Christian—probably quite religious—but at least she was not an evangelist. He could make up his own mind about this whole God thing when he was older. He didn't plan on dying any time soon.

His eyes turned towards the men lying on their cots. He knew that none of them planned on dying now, either, but here they were, knocking hard on death's door.

With no warning at all, Martha began to laugh.

"What's so funny?" Byron asked.

Martha continued laughing as she asked him, "Do you know how Sawbill Landing got its name?"

"No," Byron said, "but I'll bet you're about to tell me."

"Have you met Hjelmer Finseth yet?" she asked.

Byron thought about the men he'd treated today, then said, "No, I don't believe so. Or maybe I have, but just didn't get his name."

"Trust me," Martha said, "if you had met him, you would know it. It isn't likely you would forget him."

"That good, huh?" Byron said, a twinkle in his eye. "So you mean you may have found a replacement for Max already?"

"I am not that kind of a woman!" she snapped back at him. "And if Hjelmer Finseth was the last man on earth, I would still not be interested in him. Not *that way*, anyhow." She stopped, bringing his appearance back into her mind. "I've never seen anyone so big!"

"Huge?" Byron asked. "Just how huge is he?"

"He's so big that he could pull the trees out of the forest with his bare hands."

"That so?" Byron asked, beginning to laugh slightly, too.

"He's so big," Martha continued, "that if you could find the tallest pine tree in the woods, he would still have to look down to see the top of it."

This brought Byron to a full-fledged belly laugh.

Some of the healthier men began to laugh softly at the image of Hjelmer standing tall in the forest, head high above the tips of the mighty pines. Soon their chuckles turned into snorts, and finally they were holding their poor, sore stomachs, groaning as they roared.

Hjelmer was just outside, and he heard his name mentioned. Everyone was still laughing when he walked into the meeting hall.

"Who's dat laughing at me?" Hjelmer growled as he walked in. "I am not a funny man!" And this made the men laugh all the harder.

"Vat ist ju laughing at?" Hjelmer demanded again.

"We're not laughing at you," said one of the men, sitting up for the first time since Martha and Byron had set foot inside the meeting hall. "It's the little lady over there. What's your name, cutie?"

"It's Martha," she answered, not sure if she should give them any more information about herself.

"Martha?" another man asked, slowly propping his elbow on his cot and placing his head on his fist. "Max's Martha?"

"Yes," Martha answered. "You knew Max?"

"Everybody knew Max," a tall, skinny young man said. "And everybody loved him. Well, you know, like a brother. He was the best."

Martha found herself wishing, oh so hard, that she had had the opportunity to get to know him, too. Even this little glimpse of the man she'd hoped to spend the rest of her life with helped.

"Tell me about him," she said as she crouched beside the man who had volunteered what little she had learned about her betrothed.

"But best of all," the too-thin young man said, after the men had all related tales about Max's kindness and consideration for the other men in the camp, "was his sense of humor. Many was the night he kept us from going crazy with his tales of life in Connecticut." He paused. "And that was your Max. He said you were the best thing God ever sent his way."

"He—he said that?" Martha asked. "But—but he didn't even know me."

"Just like you didn't know him," one of the others said. "But look, here you are. And from what I hear tell, you're a stubborn sort. They say you aren't going to leave us."

"No," Martha said, strangely feeling like she was home—where she belonged. No, you couldn't pry her away from here now for anything.

Byron listened, fascinated, and watched the men, one by one, come to life right before his eyes. It was like she had some strange, magical power over them.

When it was once again silent, he said to Martha, "You were going to tell me how Sawbill Landing got its name before you got sidetracked with Max. So, do I get to hear the secret?"

"Tisn't no secret," Hjelmer said, his voice booming. "It all started ven I vent in to Hibbing to see vhy ve hadn't been getting no mail."

The men all sat, smiling at Hjelmer's tale, even though they'd heard it countless times before.

"Vell, de postman, he said he didn't know vere to send it. I told him yust to send it to the Landing, and he asked me 'Vich landing is dat?'"

He sat and waited as the men listened intently. "'It's da landing vere da sawmill is,' I told him. Only I couldn't help it dat I'd come down mit a really bad cold, so ven I said *Sawmill* it sounded like *Sawbill.* So, he's been sending da mail out here to Sawbill Landing ever since."

The men all laughed, as did Martha and Byron. As they sat chatting with one another, almost as if they had never been sick at all, Byron pulled Martha towards the door.

When they stepped outside, the storm Byron had predicted had arrived in full fury. The snow was whirling wildly through the air, and the wind grew stronger even as they watched.

In spite of the weather, Byron pulled her close and hugged her. "Thank you."

"You're welcome," she said, "but for what?"

"I don't know what you just did in there, but if I were a betting man I would lay you odds that by morning every one of those men will be ready to go out with an ax over their shoulder to start back to work."

She looked up at him with a smile warm enough to melt the snow before it hit the ground.

"What's your secret?" he asked.

"Come," she said. "I'll show you." She pulled him by the hand back inside the meeting hall. The men were still talking and laughing. She took him over to the spot where she had set her Bible.

"While you were gone, I read this." She handed the Bible to him and pointed to Proverbs 17:22.

"A merry heart doeth good like a medicine," he read aloud.

"Well, Dr. Martha," he said, "congratulations! Looks like you found the right prescription."

"Yes," she said. "Me and God."

CHAPTER SIX

Byron decided to sleep in the meeting hall with the men, even though many of them appeared well on the road to recovery. Maya invited Martha to move in with her and the children. It was, she convinced Martha, a godsend for her, as it was terribly lonely, especially at night since Uno had died.

Martha started when she heard the clock on the table chime three bells. The two women had been talking for hours, like longtime friends who had not seen each other for years. "I think we'd better get some sleep," Martha said. "You probably have to get up early to prepare breakfast for the men."

"Six o'clock," Maya said, yawning and stretching. "You're right. That's only three hours away."

They retired to the double bed, probably the only one in the entire camp, and had almost fallen asleep when Martha began softly giggling.

"Martha?" Maya asked quietly. "What is it?"

"I don't know," she answered. "Well, not exactly." Martha struggled to keep her voice down so she wouldn't wake the children. "I came here to marry Max, even though he hadn't asked me. Well, not in so many words. But his poems—oh, Maya, they were so beautiful." Her laughter turned to tears. "I just wish I could have known him. I mean *really* known him, not just in letters."

"He was a wonderful man," Maya said, rubbing her new friend's back, trying to ease the pain. "I know you would have liked—*loved* him—in time."

"Do you really think so?" Martha asked. She sat up in the bed. "Then I seem to have a real problem."

Maya waited, and when Martha didn't continue she asked, "Which is…?"

"My problem is Byron—Dr. Ferguson," Martha said, finding it strange to even say his name. "Just yesterday we were total strangers, yet I feel I have known him all my life."

Again Martha made Maya wait.

"Maybe it is just that I admired him so in his dedication to the sick men." She hesitated. "My father was a doctor. I saw him labor over complete strangers many times. But never, ever did he seem as intent on curing them as Byron did today."

Now Maya laughed. "Do you think you are falling in love with him?" she asked.

"I don't think so. I don't know. I can't be! I hardly know him."

"And that is a problem?" Maya asked. "I don't see how."

Martha shook her head so hard Maya could hear it in the darkness. "You can't learn to love somebody in just a day."

"That's what my mama told me, too," Maya said, "but in just three days Uno and I were married and on our way to a new country."

Martha gasped. "Weren't you scared?"

"No. I knew as long as I was with Uno, everything would be all right. No! Not all right! It would be wonderful!"

"And you never regretted it?"

"Never," Maya said. "We lived in Michigan first, and four of the children were born there. Then we came here to Sawbill Landing, and the last two were born here." She sighed. "I just wish your Dr. Ferguson had been here then. I didn't have a midwife, or a doctor, or anything. Only Uno."

Martha felt a thrill run through her at the sound of Maya calling Byron *your Dr. Ferguson*. How foolish! He was no more hers than she was Max's.

"I'm so glad you are here," Maya said, yawning again. "It has been so long since I have had a woman to talk to."

"I like it, too," Martha said, "but now we really do have to get to sleep or neither of us will be worth anything when it's time to get up."

The clock in the kitchen struck one soft *ding* to mark the half hour. In a matter of minutes both women drifted off to sleep.

* * *

In the meeting hall Byron Ferguson lay on his cot, listening to the almost peaceful sounds of the men who had been so restless just hours earlier. Was there really something to Martha's verse?

He smiled. *Martha's verse!* He remembered going to Sunday school every week in the little church in the Ohio town where he grew up. "Claim that verse as your own." He could almost hear Rev. Faulkner giving the admonition. Was it possible? If a certain verse applied to the situation, could you really believe it was for your own personal use?

As he pondered the things of God, for the first time in many years, he waged a battle with his private demons: demons of indifference, hatred, selfishness, and of greed.

He'd become a doctor because they made good money. Oh, yes, the idea of helping sick people had its merits, but that wasn't the main reason he'd become a physician. Of course he'd never counted on the disruption caused by that awful thing called a war. He had seen the worst of the worst when it came to suffering. Men—no, *boys* who should still have been at home with their mothers and fathers—died hopelessly on the battlefields. Men who had responsibilities to their families at home were piled in heaps, buried in huge holes with other men thrown on top of them; they would never fulfill those responsibilities. It was enough to make any man bitter. It certainly was enough to make one wonder about the love of God.

He smiled as he thought of Martha's verse. How long had it been since he'd had a merry heart? He recalled his days as a child, when he and his brothers would get into mischief, looking for some poor innocent victim to their pranks, and they would laugh. He wondered if he could ever be happy again.

Until today, he thought. And here he was, in the middle of a little logging camp, setting up a medical practice. Granted, it probably wouldn't last more than a few days, but for however long it did, he knew he would not be paid for his services. Not much, anyway, and not for some time to come. The men would not have any cash until they sold their logs in the spring, and this was just November. So much for his guilty feelings over greed. Monetary gain was certainly out of the picture for now.

His mind tripped over an image of Martha again. She had worked right alongside him, tending to the men at the camp. Surely she had not bargained for what she found. But it didn't dampen her spirits any. If this was a war, and maybe it was—of its own kind—she would have been what they called a real trooper.

Finally, in desperation and unsure of himself, he began to pray. "God, I hope you still remember who I am. I know I've sort of forgotten about you, so if you don't, I understand." He felt a load lift off his back, "I think I need your help." He smiled. "You see, Martha thinks we can make all these men well just by making them laugh. Well, I'm sorry, God, but you see, I've become a doctor. We do things a little different from that. So, if you have some other way—some *medical way*—to help these men, I'd sure like to know what it is." He stopped, thought several moments, then ended with "I'm sorry I've been gone for so long. I'll try to stick closer this time." As an afterthought he added, "Amen."

He slid his hand along the cot and felt Martha's leather bag. He assumed she would have taken it to Maya's with her. He reached inside, feeling guilty for invading her privacy, until he found what he wanted. He pulled her Bible out and went to the small window, feeling his way until he could see the moonlight reflecting off the newly fallen snow.

He thumbed through the pages until his eyes rested on a passage in Isaiah. *"When the poor and needy seek water, and there is none, and their tongue faileth for thirst, I the Lord will hear them, I the God of Israel will not forsake them. I will open rivers in high places, and fountains in the midst of the valleys: I will make the wilderness a pool of water, and the dry land springs of water. I will plant in the wilderness the cedar, the shittah tree, and the myrtle, and the oil tree; I will set in the desert the fir tree, and the pine, and the box tree together: that they may see, and know, and consider, and understand together: that they may see, and know, and consider, and understand together, that the hand of the Lord hath done this."*

He shook his head in disbelief. Could God be talking to him? Was it really that simple? He went back to his cot and laid down, knowing that at least he'd be able to sleep peacefully while he waited for morning, and for the spring he knew must be nearby.

"Thank you," he said just before he drifted off, and he knew that his gratitude was twofold: towards both God and Martha.

As he slept, he dreamed of springwater running over rocks in the middle of the snow. Streams of living water kept echoing in his head like Swiss yodels in the Alps. He knew, even in his state of unconsciousness, that if he could just find the water from the spring...

CHAPTER SEVEN

In the morning the wind was still howling. Martha looked around the little tarpaper shack for a window, and seeing none, went to the door and cracked it just a smidgen to look outside. The snow, light and fluffy, swirled in the air.

She hurried to slam the door shut before the winter blizzard attacked her. Never, in all of her life, had she seen a storm as fierce as this in Boston. She longed to be back there, then was faced with the reality that her parents and her home were all gone, so she might as well be content to stay where she was.

Her mind switched to Byron. He had been tending the men all night. He must be exhausted. She had to get to the meeting hall to relieve him so he could get a few hours sleep.

Martha grabbed her heavy black wool coat from the hook on the wall. Pulling the thick fur collar tight up against her cheeks, she opened the door again.

"Where do you think you are going?" Maya asked her.

"I have to get over to help Byron," she said. "He needs me."

"I'm sure he probably does," Maya said, "but you won't do him any good wandering alone in such weather."

"Then find one of the men to go with me," Martha said, making it sound easy.

"I'm not going out in this either. We will just have to wait until they come to us."

"And how long do you think that will take?"

"Long enough for the smell of the salt pork and flapjacks to wake up their stomachs," Maya said.

Martha sniffed the air. Maya was absolutely right. It did smell good. And she was hungry.

Soon the men began arriving, two by two, to fill their stomachs. "No work today," they remarked one after the other. "Can't hardly see your hand in front of your face out there."

"Have you seen Dr. Ferguson?" Martha asked each one.

The answer was always the same. "No."

The men gathered around the long plank table in Maya's shack while Maya heaped flapjacks on their plates, and they ate like it was their last meal. Between bites—well, almost, Martha thought—they talked. The weather, of course, was the major topic of the conversation. Finally one of the men asked, "Where's Hjelmer?"

It was odd, Martha realized, that the biggest man in camp was missing. He didn't seem like the type who was apt to miss a meal—for anything or anyone.

"He didn't go out in the storm, did he?" one of the lumberjacks asked. "Even Hjelmer couldn't survive very long out in this."

"Maybe we should form a party and go out to hunt for him," another one suggested. "If we all go together..."

"No!" Maya insisted. "It's far too dangerous. Besides, don't you see? Wherever Hjelmer is, it's likely Dr. Ferguson is with him. They are both missing."

"She's right," one of the men said. "If Hjelmer gets hurt, at least the doc can see to him."

"Yeah," another said, "unless the doc is hurt, too. He's not used to the woods like Hjelmer."

"Then Hjelmer could pick him up like a sack of flour and carry him home." The men laughed, but Martha's stomach flip-flopped and jumped right into her throat. Nothing could happen to Byron. Max had tried to help the sick men in camp and now Max was dead. Suppose Byron had found a way to help them, too, but it cost him his life?

Soon the men went back to laughing, seeming to forget about the two missing members of the camp. Their voices buzzed in Martha's ears, blocking her concentration. What could she do to help? She knew it would be foolish to go out looking for them by herself. If the men thought Hjelmer couldn't survive out there, it was a sure thing that she would never make it.

"Oofta! But is it ever cold out dere!" Hjelmer said as he stamped into Maya's shack, snow flying off his huge black boots in every direction. "Hope you got some good hot coffee, Maya," he said, plopping down on the split log bench so hard that the other end flew up in the air, knocking him onto the floor with a loud *thud!*

Martha went over and offered him a hand to get back up, which sent the whole group into hysterics. Hjelmer pulled on her hand, but the only thing it accomplished was for Martha to land on top of him, causing even more laughter.

"Was Byron with you?" she asked, oblivious to the roar of the men.

"Byron?" Hjelmer asked, rubbing his head where she had hit it on her way down. "Oh, you mean da good doctor? Ya, he vas vit me."

"So where is he?" Martha asked, staring at him, desperate to bore holes into his brain to learn the answers she so desperately wanted.

"He's coming in a couple of minutes," Hjelmer said. "He vanted to stop off at da sick house first."

"He's all right?" Martha asked, letting out a sigh that sounded like the howling wind outside. "He didn't...die?"

"Of course not," Hjelmer said. "I vudn't let that happen."

"Not if you could help it," Martha said, half-heartedly agreeing with the Swedish giant.

"It vas da craziest ting," Hjelmer said. "He came to me early dis morning. Vay before daybreak, it vas." He rubbed his head again. "He asked me if I knew vare dare vas a spring."

"A spring?" Martha asked. "In the winter?"

"Ya, sure," Hjelmer said. "Ya know, a spring never freezes, no matter how cold it gets. That's vat the good doctor vas countin' on."

"You found a spring?" Martha asked in disbelief.

"Ya, I knew var it vas," Hjelmer said. "Even in dis vether, ju can't hide nothin' from Hjelmer." He roared a deep, throaty laugh. "Nope, Hjelmer is too smart for anybody."

"What did Byron want with a spring?" Martha asked.

"He said da vater vould make the men all right again," Hjelmer said, expecting it to make sense to Martha, even though it made none at all to him.

"He brought water back with him?" Martha asked.

"Ya, sure, ya betcha he did. A whole barrel full of it. Made me pull it all the vay up there empty and then all the vay back vit it plum full. Oofta! You'd of thought I vas a horse or an ox, the way he pushed me all the way back to camp."

"Take me to him," Martha insisted, her eyes pleading with Hjelmer.

"Ya, sure," he said, "yust as soon as I finish my flapjacks. A vorkin' man needs somethin' to keep him runnin'. I can't do it vithout some food." Martha watched, her eyes nearly bulging out of her head, as Hjelmer piled a dozen plate-sized pancakes onto his dish and poured nearly the whole pitcher of syrup onto them, spilling over the sides and dripping onto the table.

She sat, silently sipping her coffee, as he ate. When his plate was empty he stood up, stretched so high she thought he was going to push the roof right off the top of the little tarpaper shack, then announced "I'm ready."

Martha followed him.

"Hang onto my coattails," he ordered her, and she did as he instructed. His giant footprints seemed a block apart as she struggled to jump from one to the next. Her mind flashed back to the snowshoes she had seen hanging on the wall at Maya's shack. *Next time,* she thought, *I'll take them.*

The snow had stopped blowing and the air was as crisp as the bacon they had had for breakfast. She squinted, trying to force her eyes to adjust to the brightness of the too-white world that enveloped her.

"Ju make it okay, ya?" Hjelmer asked.

Panting, Martha said, "I'll be just fine." She waited a few seconds then asked, "How much farther is it?" It was amazing how such a short distance could seem so long now.

"It's right there," Hjelmer said, pointing just ahead of them.

Martha blinked as she took in the longhouse. It seemed so much larger than it did yesterday. Maybe it was just because it was the first time she had caught a really good glimpse of it.

Hjelmer held the door open for her and she eased her way in quietly. To her surprise, she found almost all of the men sitting up on their cots and talking cheerfully with one another. It was such a marked difference she could hardly believe her eyes.

"What happened?" Martha asked Byron as she hurried towards him.

"It's a miracle," he said, smiling at her, his eyes dancing with glee as he teased her. "I think it must be your medicine. See how they're laughing?"

"Ya, sure," Hjelmer said. "Her laughing and jur water."

"You gave them the spring water?" Martha asked.

"You know about it?" Byron asked, glaring at Hjelmer.

"Ju didn't say nothing about not saying nothing," he said to Byron, shrugging his huge overgrown shoulders.

"No," Byron said, "I guess I didn't. Okay, so the secret is out."

"But why?" Martha asked, her curiosity getting the best of her.

"Because of this," he said, picking up her Bible and opening to the page he had marked so carefully with the lacy tatted bookmark during the night. "I hope you don't mind my borrowing it." She thought she saw the hint of a blush as he added, "I—I don't know where mine is."

Martha smiled back at him. "Any time you'd like to use it," she said, "feel free."

"Thanks," he said, turning away from her as she read the passage.

"And from this you learned…" she asked, not understanding it at all.

"It's as clear as the cute little button nose on your face," he said, poking it with his finger. "God said the men needed springs of living water. So, I got Hjelmer to take me to the spring to get some of the water for them."

Just then one of the men started running for the door, nearly knocking them over as he sprinted between them. He raced outside, followed by several of the other men.

Byron began to laugh uproariously. "Well, I guess that explains that."

Martha shook her head. "Explains what?"

"Well, most of them haven't had much to eat, so when they drank all that water it cleaned them out. Or at least it started to. I hope the outhouses don't run over!"

Martha giggled, putting her hand over her mouth. It was, she had to admit, funny. She laughed a little harder, then as more of the men ran outside, she joined him in his roaring laughter.

"I would never have thought of that."

"Me either. But God did."

"And some people think God isn't practical!" Martha quipped. "A lot they know!"

"Amen!" Byron said, moving out of the way as another man raced for the door.

"Oh, by the way," Martha said, "Maya has breakfast waiting for you at her place."

"Guess I'll be on my way," he said. "That trek through the snow really made me hungry."

"Bet the men will be hungry before long, too," Martha said, laughing again. "Looks like their stomachs will be mighty empty in a hurry."

They walked outside and Byron offered his arm to her. "Wouldn't want you to fall," he said, making it sound like an excuse to be near her.

As Martha slipped her arm through his, she could have sworn she felt a flash of lightening course through her entire body. Funny how much it had warmed up in just a few minutes.

CHAPTER EIGHT

The following morning Martha found Byron sitting on his cot, watching the men as they moved about easily while they prepared to go out to work in the woods.

"Good morning, Miss Tinker," he said, nonchalantly.

"Good morning, Dr. Ferguson," she replied, just as coolly. "And did you get a good night's sleep?"

"Actually, I did," he said, sounding surprised by this revelation. "The men seem to be well on the way to recovery." He paused, then added, "Thank you."

"Me?" Martha asked. "But I didn't do anything."

"On the contrary. You began by making them laugh. You gave them something to hope for." He smiled at her so warmly she thought the snow outside must be melting. "You were wonderful medicine for them."

"Don't forget your spring water," she teased. "That was your idea."

"Well, not exactly," he admitted. "I told you God showed me that verse."

"Okay, so God did the miracles. We just sort of stood by and let Him reach down to the men."

"I like the way you draw pictures," Byron said.

"I don't draw well at all," she said, puzzled.

"Oh, yes you do," Byron insisted. "You paint beautiful pictures with your words."

"They were God's words."

"Okay, I concede," Byron said. He pulled her down on the cot beside him. "Do you know how long it has been since I've talked to God?" he asked, his face suddenly sullen.

She did not answer, but sat, waiting, listening, for him to continue.

"I was in the war," he explained. "I saw so much killing and ugliness, I thought God didn't exist. He couldn't! Not and let so many innocent men—young men—suffer like they did."

"And you blamed God for the war?" she asked.

He nodded silently.

"I did the same thing when my parents died," she said. "Then I realized that He didn't cause the fire; the candle did."

Suddenly Byron began laughing. "So God didn't cause the war? I see! The men who shot the guns—they caused it!" He turned serious again. "When I saw you turn to the Bible for an answer to the men's sickness… You really believed that God would come right down and talk to you!"

"And He did," she said. "Just like He did to you. Nobody else would have thought of going out after clean, fresh springwater and have it wash the poison right out of the men's system."

They laughed together. "We make quite a team, don't we?" he asked her, reaching over and taking her hand in his.

"We do indeed," she said. "You, me, and God." She studied him carefully, then asked "Are you sorry I came along with you? You know, if I had listened to you I would still be back in Hibbing."

"Not on your life," he said. "If I ever tell you to leave me again, kick me."

His response surprised Martha. She wondered if he was beginning to feel about her the way she did about him. *You hardly know the man*, she reminded herself, then thought about Maya and Uno. If it could work for them, why not for her and Byron?

In an effort to lighten the mood she told him, "Stand up!"

Byron cocked an eyebrow at her. Whatever was she up to now? But he did as she asked.

Martha rose from the cot as well, went behind him and then kicked him softly on the behind.

"Hey!" he said, rubbing the spot as though he had been mortally injured. "What was that for?"

"That was just in case you decide you don't need me any more. Just following orders, sir!" she snapped, saluting him. Again they laughed.

* * *

The day wore on, Byron checking on the men who had decided to wait one more day before returning to work, and Martha helping Maya with the laundry and the cooking.

By the time it was dark and the men had returned, Martha knew she could not leave now if she wanted to. There was something about Sawbill Landing that screamed "home" to her.

As she looked around at the meager surrounding in Maya's shack, she smiled at the contrast of her past life. She had never imagined that she would be in the likes of such a place. She tried to imagine the young ladies from her finishing school class peeking in on her. This certainly was not what she was trained to do, but it felt so right.

Her mind returned to the days and hours she had spent with her father down on the docks in Boston. Maybe this was her *forte* in life. She smiled. Her father would be proud of her. It was, despite his station in life, exactly the way he had trained her. Nothing was more important to her father than his fellow man, no matter how much or how little he had. Yes, if she could help make the life for these lumberjacks just a little easier, she had found her true calling in life. If God should be so good as to make Dr. Byron Ferguson a part of the package, who was she to argue?

* * *

Byron helped the two women carry food to the meeting house.

"I think I could learn to like this," Maya commented as they trekked through the snow. "To have another woman in the camp—and a doctor! And one who is not afraid to work, even!"

Byron stumbled on a tree stump which lay hidden beneath the snow, but he managed to catch his footing and kept the kettle of boiled rabbit from spilling.

"Be careful," Maya warned. "If you spill that, we might have to use the leftovers. And they might have some mushrooms in there."

"No!" Byron shouted. "God save us from any more mushrooms!"

* * *

Everyone chatted gaily as they sat around the long tables in the mess hall. There were far too many men to fit into Maya's little shack now that they all seemed to have an appetite to equal that of a bull moose.

When the men had finished eating, Byron said, "Okay, who is going to help clean up?"

"Humph!" one of the men grumbled. "That is woman's work!"

The others made similar comments until Hjelmer got to his feet. He had to stoop over to keep his head from hitting the beams on the ceiling. He said nothing, but began clearing the dishes off the table and stacking them in the big pots which were now completely empty.

"Come on," Hjelmer said. "Let's go to Maya's and ve vill vash dem."

The men began to follow his lead. They all knew better than to argue with Hjelmer. After all, without Hjelmer none of them would have a job, or a place to live, or anything else that mattered in their lives.

* * *

Maya and Martha sat at the table, drinking coffee, after the men cleared out. By the time they finished their conversation, Martha knew more about the men in camp than she knew about all of her friends back in Boston.

"And where do they all live?" she asked Maya, who drew a simple map of the logging camp on a piece of paper and labeled each one with the appropriate man's names.

"It's been a long day," Martha said, stretching and yawning. "I'm sorry I kept you up so late last night."

"You mean this morning?" Maya asked, laughing.

"Okay, this morning," Martha said, poking playfully at her new friend. "What do you say we retire early tonight?"

"Retire?" Maya asked. "I thought only old people did that."

Martha grinned. "*Retire* is also another word for *going to bed*," she explained.

"I swear I will never understand this English language!" she sputtered. "Finnish is so much easier."

"For you, maybe," Martha said. "But I could never learn it."

"Good idea, anyway," Maya said, sitting down on the bed to remove her boots and heavy woolen socks. "You know, you should borrow some of my clothes," she suggested. "Yours are nice, but they are not really what you need out here in the back woods." She leaned forward and pulled a drawer out from under the bed. She took out a pair of heavy black trousers, a buffalo plaid shirt and a pair of socks. "Try these on in the morning," she said.

"Thank you," Martha said, accepting them gracefully but wondering how she would look in such garb. She had *never* worn trousers, not even when riding. And these looked like *men's* trousers! But, she had to admit, she had been cold all day long, even with the fire burning in the tiny shack.

"Good night," she said as she pulled the blankets tightly up around her neck after she had gotten into her nightgown.

"Good night," Maya answered. The two women were sound asleep in seconds.

* * *

Across the camp, Byron crawled onto his cot in the long house. It seemed so small when they first arrived—crammed full of sick and near dying men. Now, alone, its size was overwhelming. He longed for a small, intimate place of his own. Although his thoughts were usually calm and orderly, tonight they began roaming uncontrollably. Try as he might, he could not get rid of the vision of any house—or shack—being invaded by the incredible Martha Tinker.

"Forget it!" he said into the stillness. He drifted off to sleep as his final thought vanished into the air: *perhaps that is the only way I will be able to find a Bible to read every day.*

CHAPTER NINE

Martha tossed and turned most of the night, her mind filled with thoughts of Byron. She tried desperately to chase them away, but echoes of Maya's story of her love for Uno kept arguing in her head. Finally, she sat up on the edge of the bed and began to pray silently.

"Dear Lord," her heart cried out, "please show me what to do. You know I am so alone and so afraid. I don't know what the future holds, and if it is your will, please let it include Byron."

Martha had not admitted, even to herself, that she felt so strongly about the doctor who had been a complete stranger just a few days ago.

She crawled back into bed and slept as soundly as a newborn baby, content in knowing that she had placed the entire matter in God's hands.

In the morning she awoke to the smell of the food Maya was preparing the men's breakfast. She knew they would begin straggling in, two by two, four by four, to get their fill of the vittles before they began the strenuous day's work.

Hjelmer and Byron came in together. Martha sat and watched the two of them talk freely, joking like they had been friends forever.

If they can be such good friends already, why can't Byron and you do the same?

She looked around, wondering who had spoken. The men were all engaged in conversation with one another, leaving only Maya, but it had not been a woman's voice. There was only one possible answer: it had been God's voice. Was it audible, or just within her own heart and soul?

"God," she prayed silently, "are you telling me it is okay for me to think of him like...like that?"

As if in answer to her unspoken question, Byron looked at her, winked and said, "You look especially lovely this morning, Martha."

Martha felt the color rise in her cheeks. She glanced down at her men's trousers and her thick plaid shirt and began to laugh. Was he teasing her? Surely he must be. She had been clad in dresses until this morning; her image now was anything but conducive to romantic thoughts.

"There is a glow about you that's been absent before," he said, making her even more uncomfortable.

"Thank you," she finally managed to mumble, turning away from him.

The conversation soon turned to Christmas. "It's only a few weeks away," one of the men said. "Who is going to be Father Christmas and take the toys to the children?"

Martha was impressed by their consideration for the children. She knew the only ones in the camp were Maya and Uno's clan. It would no doubt be a very difficult season this year—their first one without a father.

"Let's all make something for them," another suggested.

Soon everyone was talking excitedly. Martha tried to join in, but her heart was not in it. For her, too, this would be a trying time. She thought of the Christmases past when she had helped the servants at home decorate the huge mansion in Boston. She could almost smell the aromas from the kitchen, with baked goods of every description filling the long tables and the goose roasting in the oven. She felt a tear slowly trickle down her cheek.

A heavy hand settled on her shoulder, startling her. She turned and looked up to see Hjelmer standing behind her.

"Come with me," he said, helping her up from her chair.

Everyone seemed to be too busy to notice them slip outside.

"I have an idea," he said, "but I need de help of a voman."

Martha laughed. It was hard to imagine that Hjelmer would ever own up to needing anyone's help for anything.

"What for?" she asked.

"Yust vait here," he said, then disappeared back inside Maya's shack. Soon he was back with Martha's black wool coat, her mittens, a warm scarf, and two sets of snowshoes. He helped her put on her coat, then waited while she wrapped the scarf around her head and her neck and stuck her delicate fingers into the mittens.

"What do I do with these?" she asked, holding the snowshoes.

"Ju have never used them?" Hjelmer asked.

Martha shook her head.

"Yust carry them to the edge of the camp," he said, holding his own pair in his hands. "Ve von't need them until ve get outside the camp."

Martha did as instructed, almost running to keep up with his giant-sized steps along the trail. Soon they were at the edge of the camp. The sun was now shining on the white snow, and the field looked like it was covered in diamonds. The branches of the evergreen trees almost touched the ground beneath the weight of the snow.

"It is like they are kneeling, no?" Hjelmer asked, standing and admiring the scene. "Like they are telling God they love Him."

The tenderness in his voice surprised her and Martha nodded in agreement, almost afraid that if she spoke it would disappear. It was, indeed, the most beautiful thing she had ever seen.

Hjelmer bent down and helped her fasten the leather straps around her boots. "Ready?"

"Ready," Martha said, taking a step. Her left snowshoe landed on top of her right one, sending her sprawling into the soft, fluffy snow. Hjelmer kept right on walking, unaware that she had fallen.

"Wait!" she called out to him. He turned back to her and took huge steps around in a circle so he could come back to rescue her.

He reached down and pulled her to her feet. He began to walk again, and once more after just one step Martha was back on the ground.

"I can't do this!" Martha cried out to him.

"Ju yust have to lift one foot ahead of the other, like this," he said, making it seem so simple when he did it.

Martha watched him lift one foot well in the air and set it off to the side slightly before he began to lift the other foot. She imitated him, and to her surprise she managed to take several steps before she went down again.

"Ve vill never make it to the tree at this rate," he said, trying hard not to laugh. But soon he was roaring hilariously at her.

Martha realized how hopeless she must appear, but she joined him in laughter instead of being hurt or embarrassed. She enjoyed their ability to relate to one another alone out here in the wilderness. She looked around, grateful that no one else had followed them. She was sure she would be humiliated if anyone else saw her.

Hjelmer slowed down and walked behind her, giving her instructions on how to use the apparatus that seemed to come so easily to him. Soon she was walking like a professional.

"'Tis good," Hjelmer said. "Ju learn quick."

"Where are we going?" Martha asked him. She smiled, realizing that she was going off into the woods with a near stranger. She could almost hear her mother scolding her and her father saying, *"You have to trust your instincts, Mama. She'll be just fine. She is a good girl."*

"I told ju," Hjelmer said. "Ve are going to the tree."

Martha laughed. "*The* tree?" she asked. "How do you know which one is *the* tree?"

"Ju vill know it ven ju see it," he said. "It is so tall it reaches all the vay to heaven."

They continued walking in silence, both watching for *the* tree. Suddenly, off in the distance, Martha saw it. He was right. It was higher than all the others. She had never seen anything so magnificent. She pointed to it and Hjelmer nodded, agreeing that it was indeed *the* tree.

When they got to the base of the mighty evergreen, they looked up...and up...and up...until they finally saw the very tip of it.

"Ve need to trim the tree," Hjelmer said.

"How are we going to get that tree back to camp to trim it?" Martha asked, still staring at the top of it. "It would take all the horses to pull it."

Hjelmer's mouth dropped open. "Ve vill not cut it!" he nearly shouted. "It has lived too many jears to kill it now." He shook his head as he said, "Ve vill trim it here."

"Here?" Martha asked. "But what good will that be? No one will see it. No one but you and me."

"And God and all His creatures," Hjelmer explained. "Ve vill put some berries on it for the birds and some acorns for the squirrels."

"And some bark for the deer," Martha said, getting caught up in the spirit of Hjelmer's tree.

"Jah!" Hjelmer said excitedly. "Now ju got it."

Soon they were finished with the entire tree, or at least as far up as they could reach. Martha held her breath as Hjelmer climbed up, branch after branch, reaching down for the items Martha gathered and handed to him. She reached up as far as she could, stretching up onto her tiptoes, hoping he would not fall.

"How does it look?" Hjelmer called down to her.

"It looks wonderful!" Martha said just as a little chickadee alit on a branch almost beside Hjelmer and pecked away at a bittersweet berry.

"Then I'm coming down," Hjelmer said. "Stand back."

Martha moved away from the tree, expecting him to climb down the same way he had gotten up—branch by branch. Instead, he landed with a tremendous *thud* beside her.

She ran to him, but he was soon up on his feet and brushing the snow off.

"Oofta!" he sputtered. "I'm not as jung as I used to vas!"

They laughed together as they headed back to camp. Martha smiled when Hjelmer said, "Jah, ju do good vit the big feet!"

Martha was amazed as she trekked back almost easily on the snowshoes. The serenity of the forest was too great to be interrupted by conversation, so she and Hjelmer walked in silence. The only sounds were those of nature itself: birds chirping gaily, chipmunks and squirrels scampering hither and yon, deer standing gracefully amidst the trees. Before long the camp was in sight.

"We're back already?" Martha asked in surprise.

"Ju don't know?" Hjelmer asked. "It is alvays twice as far to someplace as it is back again."

Martha pondered this, then agreed. "I never thought about it before," she said, "but you are right."

"Of course I am right," Hjelmer said. "Hjelmer is alvays right!" He turned around to look at Martha. "Hjelmer is right about something else," he said.

Finally, after she didn't question him, he asked, "Vell, aren't ju going to ask me vat else I am right about?"

"Okay," Martha conceded. "What else are you right about?"

"The good doctor," Hjelmer said. "He likes ju. Jah, he likes ju a lot."

Martha smiled, in spite of her efforts not to. "He, um, he just likes everybody. He's a doctor. He *has* to like everybody."

"Dat might be true," Hjelmer said, "but he likes ju in a vay dat he doesn't like everybody."

"You are just imagining things," Martha said. Almost before the words were out of her mouth, they were accosted by Byron.

"Where have you been?" he asked, his eyes filled with fear and concern. "I've been worried sick about you."

Hjelmer laughed. "If the good doctor gets sick, den vat vill ve all do?"

"I didn't mean *sick* sick," Byron said. "I mean scared silly sick. Now, will you please tell me where you've been?"

"I guess so," Martha said, chuckling. "But I didn't know I had to answer to you for every move I make. You know Hjelmer wouldn't let anything happen to me."

"And I was supposed to know that you were with Hjelmer?" Suddenly, the thought of what Hjelmer might have done to her out in the middle of the woods dawned on him.

"Did you hurt her?" he yelled at the big Swede.

"Don't worry," Martha said, smiling warmly at his implications. "He was a perfect gentleman."

"Ja, sure," Hjelmer said, "except for the part var I fell down on the ground from up in the tree. I didn't look much like a gentleman lying there all sprawled out from here to eternity."

"You fell out of a tree?" Byron asked. "What were you doing up in a tree?"

"I cannot tell ju jet," Hjelmer said, throwing a look Martha's way which defied her to share their secret with anyone else. "But soon ju vill know. Ja, soon. Very soon."

Martha winked at him, signaling that she understood that it was not time now to reveal their little project. When Hjelmer said the time was right, she knew he would reveal *the* tree to everyone in camp.

CHAPTER TEN

Soon cheer and good tidings filled the entire camp. The Koski children put forth their best behavior with the promise of a visit by Father Christmas. With all the extra help with the daily chores, Maya even found time to relax. Her favorite pastime, from childhood days, had been reading, but her English was so limited she could not understand the old newspapers the men brought to her. In their newly gained spare time, Martha helped her with English, using the Bible as their textbook. Eager to learn, Maya made a perfect student.

Early one morning Martha awoke to find Maya and the children all gathered at the table. Maya was helping each of the children, even little three-year-old Robert, form letters into words on a piece of birch bark. Martha smiled, realizing that she had indeed been able to make a difference in Sawbill Landing.

Maya looked up at her, smiling back. "I will so hate to have you leave," she said.

Martha jumped. The thought of leaving this place, which had become a haven to her, had long since fled from her mind. She was home, and she fully intended to stay.

"Why would I leave? Are you saying you don't want me here any more?"

"No!" Maya protested. "I would love for you to stay forever, but I just assumed that with Byron going into Hibbing tomorrow, you would accompany him."

"Byron is going to Hibbing?" Martha asked, her heart feeling like it sank clear to her toes. Why hadn't he said anything to her? She had assumed that he was as happy here as she was. They had gotten so close over the past few weeks, she could not imagine her life without him. Was he returning to a medical practice somewhere? Why hadn't he mentioned it to her? He had seemed so open with her. He had shared childhood memories with her, had told her stories about the war that she was sure he had never shared with anyone else. He had even confessed his lack of faith, and she thought she had helped him back to a place of trust. As she pondered every word of their conversations, which were indelibly etched on her heart, she realized that he had not once talked about his future. What plans did he have? Was she foolish to think—or at least hope—she would be a part of them?

As if on cue, he walked in with Hjelmer.

"Morning, ladies," he said, offering them a sweeping bow. "You, too, Missy," he said to little Patricia, as he tousled her blond curls. "It's a fine, clear day for a trip. Perhaps I should leave today, rather than risk waiting until tomorrow. Think we can get some breakfast early?"

Martha tried to speak, but the lump in her throat grew. The words would not bypass it. Instead, a tear trickled down her cheek. She hurried to turn away from him. How could she have been so foolish? So utterly stupid? What right did she have to try to put a claim on the handsome, stubborn, frustrating, but lovable doctor?

The thoughts whirred inside her head. When had he become so important to her? She knew she had no rights to him, but her heart said differently. Somehow, he had managed to become an important part of her life, almost from the moment they met at the hotel in Hibbing. Now he was all she had. She had found a haven with him, and she wasn't about ready to forsake that place now. He could beg all he wanted to, but he couldn't just walk out of her life that easily.

"You can't leave!" she said, turning to face him with every ounce of courage she could muster. "Not now, not ever!" She sat down, realizing from his expression that she had surprised both of them. She had a mind of her own, and he knew that, but this was overly forceful, even for Martha.

"What are you talking about?" Byron asked, his bright eyes twinkling with merriment.

Those eyes! Martha thought. *They could melt the biggest icicle in the entire north woods.*

"You didn't tell me you were leaving," she said accusingly. "You were just going to ride out of camp, out of my life, without telling me? Without even saying goodbye?"

Byron laughed. Martha glared at him, but her anger softened. Whenever he laughed, she knew he could do anything he wanted to and she could not stop him. That laugh had her captivated. It was, she mused, one of his most endearing qualities.

"You thought I was leaving for good?" he asked.

"You aren't?" Martha said, beginning to feel foolish.

"Of course not," he replied. "Unless you wanted to return to civilization."

Martha gulped. Was he saying that he would be willing to leave—or to stay—depending on her whims? Was it possible that he had come to love her, as she was sure she had grown to love him?

"No!" Martha cried out. "I have never been happier than I am right here. I want to stay here forever." *With you,* her heart added.

"Then it's settled," Byron said. "I will leave as soon as I get some food in me to keep me warm on the trip. I'll return tomorrow, weather permitting."

Maya, who had been hurrying to fry venison sausage and flapjacks for them, set the plates, piled high, in front of them.

"How can I be sure you'll come back?" Martha asked, the words slipping out before she could stop them.

"If you are really that worried," Byron said, "I'll take Hjelmer with me. You know I could not get away from him."

"That's a wonderful idea!" Martha exclaimed. She knew if Hjelmer went into Hibbing, there was no way he would fail to return to Sawbill Landing. It was his life. It was everything he held dear. She knew if Hjelmer went with him, Byron *would* be back. More importantly, it wasn't a good idea to go alone in the unpredictable winter weather. "Would you accompany the doctor into Hibbing? Please?"

When Hjelmer laughed, it was as if every tree in the forest trembled. "I had already told the good doctor that he could not go alone, and that I vud go vit him," he said, spoiling the fun the doctor was having teasing Martha.

Martha looked down, embarrassed that she had shown such little confidence in Byron. Of course he knew it was far too dangerous to make such a trip alone. He knew the back woods of northern Minnesota far better than she did, yet her instincts told her that it was indeed dangerous. But if anybody could bring her Byron back, she knew it was Hjelmer.

Martha blushed. Her mind flitted back to the day Maya had called him "her Byron." Was it contagious? It was the first time she had truly admitted to herself that to her that was exactly what he had become: *Her Byron!* The very breath of her life. It seemed almost impossible that they had known each other such a short time, but then she thought of Maya and Uno. Was it possible that she and Byron might one day share that same deep love for one another? Or did they already possess it?

As Byron took the last bite of food from his plate, he stood up and said to Hjelmer, "Well, shall we get started? It's a good ride into town. We don't want to have to stay more than one day. Christmas is a comin' and the goose is gettin' fat," he sang to the English carol.

Martha chuckled. She knew what she would do while he was gone. It was the perfect thing to occupy her time until he returned. Oh, yes, this was going to be a very good Christmas.

* * *

Maya and Martha stood at the tiny doorway of the shanty and watched as Hjelmer and Byron, each astride their horse, waved goodbye. They waved back at them, and called out, "Hurry home."

"We have a lot to do while they are gone," Martha said. "Do you have any extra flour?"

"Of course. The men always see that we have more than enough before the winter sets in. What else do you need?"

"Sugar?"

"Yes," Maya replied, "although not a lot. I don't use it very often." Suddenly her eyes lit up as bright as the candles on the Christmas trees of Martha's bygone days in Boston. "I have something very special."

She scurried over to the cupboard and pulled the bottom bin open. She reached way down into it, then pulled her flour-covered arm back out. In her hand she held a cheesecloth-wrapped parcel, which she carried to the table. She slowly unwrapped it, and several chunks of a deep rich brown substance clunked onto the wooden planks.

"What is that?" Martha asked.

"It is my Christmas present from Uno," she said, her eyes overflowing with tears. "He didn't know I saw him put it there, before…" She could not continue.

Martha went to her and put her arms around her, drawing her friend into a warm embrace.

"It's…" Maya said, stammering, "it's maple sugar. He made it for me last spring when the sap was running. He told me he had something very special for me, but he wouldn't tell me what it was. I saw him by the cupboard one day. He heard me, so he slammed the bin shut and turned around to face me, a grin from ear to ear on his face. When I asked him what he was doing he said, 'Nothing.' But his arms were covered with flour…"

"Just like yours are now," Martha said, laughing.

Maya brushed the white powder off her red and black wool shirt. Through her tears, she too laughed. "Yes, just like mine."

"So you went to investigate?" Martha asked.

"Yes," Maya confessed. "But only after he went out to the woods. I didn't want him to know I had found out his secret. I didn't want to spoil his surprise." She paused. "Ever since I have been a little girl, I could never stand surprises. I had to know what Santa Claus was bringing me. He always seemed to come early, and one year when my mother discovered that I had found the presents, she explained that he had to visit some homes early, or he would not be able to get the gifts to everyone on time."

"And you believed her?"

"Oh, yes! She said if I ever did that again that he would not leave any gifts for me." Maya smiled. "And I never looked for presents ahead of time again. Not until this year…"

Maya went to the drawer and took out a large knife. She pushed with all her might on the brown block until a piece finally broke loose.

"Here," she said, handing it to Martha. "Try it. It is the most heavenly taste."

"No, you eat it," Martha said, refusing to take it. "It is yours—from Uno."

Maya cut another piece off. "Okay, we will do it together," she said, holding one piece to her own mouth and handing the other piece to Martha.

"Okay," Martha said. "On the count of three. One, two, three…"

Both women bit into the sugar at the same instant. "Umm," Maya said.

"Ooh," Martha agreed. "You are right. It is wonderful! It would be perfect in cookies."

The two women sat at the table, like sisters, and ate one bite after another. Before they knew it, they had consumed the entire block.

Maya put the knife up to carve off another sliver. "Oh, my!" she exclaimed. "I can't believe we ate the whole thing!"

"We did?" Martha asked, her face registering surprise. "It was just so good, I couldn't stop…"

"Now, what were you asking about sugar for?" Maya asked.

The two women sat, laughing, and that's the way they were when the men arrived for breakfast. For the first time since Maya had arrived in camp, there was nothing prepared for the men to eat.

"I'll have some oats cooked for you in five minutes," she said, scurrying to get the big kettle and dump the water from the bucket into it. She took it to the pot-belly stove and set it on the platform on top of it, praying that it would heat faster than usual.

Martha went to the cupboard and got out bowls.

"All we are having is oats?" one of the men grumbled. "And that is supposed to last us all day in the woods?"

"My grandfather back in the old country used to say that if you had a good bowl of oats, it would stick to your ribs all day. So, yes, in honor of my grandfather at Christmas time, you are eating oats today."

She went to the stove and dumped the oats into the kettle. "Thank you," she whispered as she looked upwards. For some reason, it was already boiling.

CHAPTER ELEVEN

By the time noon rolled around, neither Maya nor Martha was the least bit hungry.

"Good thing we packed lunches for the men," Maya said.

"It sure is," Martha said, quick to agree. "I don't think I could possibly look food in the face."

Maya laughed. "Food doesn't have a face," she said, looking puzzled.

"We could have carved faces into that maple sugar," Martha said.

"Yes, but we wouldn't want to eat our friends," Maya joked. "It would be like we were…" she groped for the word she wanted.

"Cannibals," Martha said.

"Cannibals," Maya repeated. "Okay, I learned my new word for today."

"I'm sure it will come in very handy, too," Martha said, giggling. She didn't know what had gotten into them, but they were both as punchy as could be.

"Suppose there was something bad in that sugar?" Martha asked.

"Don't think so," Maya replied. "If there was something bad in it, I wouldn't feel as good as I do now."

"You're right," Martha said, still not too sure of it. She had heard about people who were drunk, but she had never really seen any of them. She had certainly never imbibed to excess herself. But, she imagined that *if* she were drunk, she would feel like she did now. Nothing mattered. Not really. It was like being in a state of euphoria. It didn't even matter if Byron didn't…

"Byron!" she shouted, then grabbed her head. The sound of her own voice made her head feel like it was going to split right down the middle. "Byron is gone!" Suddenly, with no warning, she was sobbing uncontrollably.

"There, there," Maya said, trying to console her, "he said he'd be back. And I do think that Byron is a man of his word."

"You think so?" Martha asked.

"I know so," Maya said. "Has he ever let you down?"

Martha began to laugh again. "Yes, he did, once—the day we got here."

"What did he do?" Maya asked.

"He let me down—off his horse," Martha said, tears rolling down her face, but now they were not tears of sorrow; they were tears from laughing so hard. "It was the best *down* I've ever had." She rocked back and forth. "He held me in his arms, almost like we were dancing."

"I've never learned to dance," Maya admitted. "Do you think you could teach me?"

"It's easy," Martha said, "but we need music." With that, the women began to sing, creating their own music. Martha got to her feet, only to fall back onto the bench by the table. "Maybe we'd better do it some other day."

"Maybe," Maya said, her own head reeling.

* * *

Byron walked into the hotel in Hibbing, causing the bell to *ding-dong* his arrival. Helga Anderson came out from the kitchen, wiping her hands on her apron. She smiled warmly when she saw him.

"You're done out at Sawbill Landing?" she asked. "How bad was it?"

"Pretty bad," Byron said, rubbing his hands together over the big black pot-belly stove that sat in the middle of the room. "Boy, it's cold out there!"

"A lot of men died?" John Anderson asked as he joined his wife.

"Too many," Byron said. "If only I could have gotten there sooner."

"But you were able to save some of them?" John asked.

"Quite a few," Byron said. "Not enough, but quite a few."

"And Miss Tinker?" John asked. "She...?" The question was left unspoken, but Byron knew immediately what he was asking.

"Oh, no!" Byron said emphatically. "She—she's just fine." He laughed as he pictured her, working side by side with him to save the lives of the men she knew nothing about.

He sobered. "I'm afraid, however, that her fiancé, Max Wilson, didn't fare as well." He hesitated, realizing again how devastating it was for Martha to learn that the only person she had any ties to in the whole world had forsaken her, even though he had no say in the matter.

"You couldn't save him?" Helga asked.

"He was already dead," Byron said. "She found him that way."

"So where is she?" Helga asked. "You dropped her off for the stage?"

"No," Byron said. "She's much too stubborn for her own good. She decided to stay in Sawbill Landing."

"Until spring?" John asked.

"Until…whenever," Byron replied. "She says she's not leaving."

"Why ever not?" John asked, scratching his head. "There's nothing to stay for, not if her man up and died."

"There's me," Byron said, grinning slyly.

"But you're here," John said. "You're surely not going back there."

"They need me," Byron said, as if that explained everything. Maybe it did. He was a compassionate man, if you looked beneath the surface. The kind that made good doctors.

"So why are you here?" John asked.

"I came to get supplies," Byron said. "Christmas supplies." He grinned again. "I figure those little kids—there's six of them, all part of one family, and they lost their daddy to this mess—they need somebody to show them some Christmas cheer. So, I decided I might as well be the one to do it."

"What do you need?" Helga asked, getting into the mood. "I have baked a lot of goodies. Take some of them back with you."

"What can I do?" John asked.

"Well, if you have a sleigh that I might borrow until just before spring thaws set in…"

"You've got it," John said. "You fixin' to take that much stuff back with you?"

"I thought I would take Martha the things she brought with her from Boston. I know she'd like to have them." He laughed. "You should see her! She's become a real lumberjack herself, all dressed up in men's wool trousers and a red and black checkered shirt that's about six sizes too big for her. She could go out in the woods with Hjelmer and fit right in."

John laughed with him, trying to picture the petite Martha Tinker standing alongside the giant Hjelmer Finseth. There wasn't a person in all Hibbing who didn't know Hjelmer Finseth; he wasn't a man you easily forgot.

"Oh, do you have a room? Hjelmer came with me, and we plan to spend the night. We'll head out early tomorrow morning. It's nice the good Lord was with us to give us such a pretty day."

John studied the doctor carefully. When Martha had said she found him an answer to her prayers, even though they weren't even uttered yet, Byron had scoffed at her. What had caused him to change his mind? Had the good doctor gone and gotten religion? And if so, where? Certainly not in the middle of a bunch of heathen men out in some logging camp!

"Of course you can have a room. Hjelmer want one, too?" Helga hurried to offer.

"We'll bunk together," Byron said. "It's cheaper that way."

Just then Hjelmer walked into the hotel lobby, letting out a yell of "Yeowch!" as his head bumped the top of the doorframe.

"Welcome," John said, extending his hand to the giant. "And Merry Christmas."

"Merry Christmas to ju, too," Hjelmer said. "It's a good one, it is."

"I'd better get busy if I'm going to find everything I want to take back with me," Byron said. "You coming along?" he asked Hjelmer.

"Ja, sure. There's not much to do here," Hjelmer said as he walked out and bumped his head again. "Damn doors!" he sputtered, rubbing the top of his head.

* * *

They made their first stop the general mercantile store. Byron walked up to the clerk and asked, "Do you have a red wool suit?"

The clerk looked him over, his eyes wandering up and down, measuring him for size.

"Nope, can't say as we do," he said. "What you want it for?"

"For Christmas," Byron said, as if that explained everything.

The clerk looked at him with a puzzled expression.

"I've got to play Santa Claus for some little kids out at Sawbill Landing," Byron explained. "From what their mother tells me, the old saint always wore a red wool suit. You don't have anything at all that might work?"

The clerk's mind raced, trying to figure out what he had that might work. He drew a complete blank. He didn't have an actual suit of any kind, and he *certainly* didn't have a red wool one. Who on earth would wear such a thing anyway?

"What you got here, Pa?" a little old lady said as she came into the store from the back room.

"Santa Claus," the clerk replied. "Can't you tell? He lost his red wool suit and he says he needs a new one by Christmas."

"But that's only a few days off," the clerk's wife said. "Not even a week. We have some fine red wool yardage, but there's hardly enough time to make a whole suit. Not by Christmas time."

She glanced around the store, her eyes pausing here and there, as she tried to figure out a feasible solution. Suddenly her eyes lit up and she almost ran to the other side of the store. "Here!" she said, grabbing something bright red and carrying it over to Byron. He looked at it, allowing it to unfold and drop open in front of him. He held it up, and discovered that she had handed him red flannel long johns! Well, they *were* red...

"Hear tell they lost a bunch of the men out there," the clerk said.

"Too many," Byron said. "But the rest of them, they're tough. They'll make it through. The little ones that need a visit from Santa Claus, they lost their father. I thought that maybe I could make it a little easier for them." He reached into his pocket for the money for the long johns. He didn't have much money left, as none of the men had been able to pay him yet for his services. He began to count it out, asking, "How much is it?"

"One dollar," the clerk answered, then groaned when his wife jabbed him in the stomach with her elbow and cleared her throat. "But since it's Christmas and all, you can have them for..."

"There ain't no charge for them," the woman said. "Why, it's downright *unChristmaslike* to charge Santa Claus for something just days before the holiday!"

"That's right," the clerk said, his face red. Byron wasn't sure if he was angry, or ashamed, but either way Byron was glad for the gift.

"The children, they'll thank you," Byron said.

The clerk wrapped it in brown paper and tied a string around it. "Merry Christmas!" he said as he handed it to Byron.

Byron wondered just how far their Christmas spirit would go, and he pondered his next move. He glanced around and saw Hjelmer sitting in a corner by the stove, playing dominos with several other men. He could always call him to help if things got out of hand. Well, he wouldn't go *too* far, but he was still doing okay, so he tried once more.

"I would like to get some candies for the children, too," he said, testing his luck just a little farther.

The woman opened the glass jars and poured a scoop of assorted candies from each one into a big white cloth bag. Then she took another bag and filled it with apples and oranges. They were expensive, as Byron knew they must have been brought up from Texas. "Go in peace," she said as she handed them to Byron, "and God be with you."

"Thank you," Byron said, motioning to Hjelmer that he was leaving.

"I'll see ju at the hotel," Hjelmer called back. "I'm vinning; I'm not gonna leave now."

"See you later," Byron said as he made an exit. He walked out into the street, pulling his hat down and his coat collar up. The wind had picked up a little, and the cold blew right through him. He looked up and down, then smiled as he saw the latest addition to the town. "Hardware" the sign said. Perfect! He knew what that meant.

He walked into the store and called out, "Anybody here?"

"Back here," came a deep male voice. Byron went in the direction of the voice and soon stood face-to-face with a man, kneeling, and a corpse. As a doctor, he knew that most hardware stores also housed the local mortuary. Fortunately, this one was no different.

The body in the coffin was that of an elderly woman. Byron smiled as he looked at her. Not only was she very dead, but she was perfect!

"Dr. Byron Ferguson," he said, extending his hand to the hardware manager, who also doubled as the mortician.

"You're a doctor?" the man asked, a smile forming on his face. "The saints be praised! It's what this town needs."

"I'm sorry to disappoint you," Byron said. "Yes, I am a doctor, but I am just here for the day. I'm returning to Sawbill Landing first thing tomorrow morning."

"Sawbill Landing?" the man asked. Byron assumed that he was new in town, or he would have heard about the logging camp.

"It's a logging camp," Byron said.

"You mean a logging camp has its own doctor, but a town like Hibbing doesn't?"

"Guess so," Byron said. "Now, just go ahead with what you were doing."

"I don't know how to do it," the man said. "Just look at this!" He grabbed the woman's hair, which was pure white and so full and bushy there was no way to control it. "She always wore it wound up tight around her head, but I can't figure out how to get it back that way. I washed it, and this is what happened."

"I think I have a solution," Byron said. "Do you have a pair of scissors?"

"Yes," the man said, getting up off the floor and going to a wooden box that contained more medical utensils than Byron had. He reached in and pulled out a pair of surgical scissors. "This do?"

"Perfect," Byron said, grabbing a big clump of the woman's hair and chopping it off. "How much do you want for it?"

"For what?" the man asked.

"The hair," Byron said.

"You want a dead woman's hair?" the man asked. "What kind of man are you, anyway?"

"I need it for Santa Claus," Byron said, making it sound perfectly logical. He proceeded to cut off more of the hair, until it was quite manageable.

"I don't know," the man said, suddenly overtaken by an urge to participate in whatever little plot this strange man who claimed to be a doctor had up his sleeve.

"If it is for the Man himself, I suppose I really can't charge you for it." He wanted to ask what he was going to do with it, but thought better of it and kept quiet.

Byron stuffed the hair into his jacket and left, thanking the man for his help. "Glad you're in town," he said as the door swung shut.

Byron walked down the street to the barber shop. He went inside and greeted the barber.

"Shave and a haircut?" the barber asked.

"Nope," Byron said. "I need a beard."

The barber laughed at him. This man was as clean-shaven as anybody he had ever seen. "It will take a while," he said. "Probably at least a good month."

"I only have a few days," Byron said, reaching into his pocket and pulling out the mass of white hair. "Can you make one out of this?"

The barber shrugged his shoulders. "Never have before, but I guess I could try. What's it for?"

"Santa Claus," Byron said, heading for the door. "I'll stop by first thing in the morning to pick it up." And he was gone, just like that, leaving the barber with a handful of long, white, fluffy hair.

* * *

Byron entered the hotel just in time to hear John Anderson tell Hjelmer, "And it's as plain as the nose on your face that he's head over heels in love with the young lady."

"Who's in love with who?" Byron asked, interrupting the twosome.

"Why you, of course," John said. "You are so in love with Miss Tinker, I doubt you can even see it yourself."

"I am?" Byron asked, shocked by the interference of near strangers into his private affairs. But he was also stunned by their assessment of the situation. Was he really that blind? Was he *in love* with Martha Tinker? The very idea of it sounded absurd. She was the most headstrong, stubborn, devoted, loving, kind, compassionate, maddening configuration of a human being that he had ever met. But, if he stopped to consider it for more than two seconds, he knew that John Anderson had seen what he was too blind to see himself: he was hopelessly, madly in love with the unpredictable, wonderful Miss Martha Tinker.

Feeling like he had been struck by lightning, he jumped. "Hjelmer," he said, "be ready to leave at the crack of dawn. We can't keep the fair lady waiting any longer." He stopped, thinking, then asked, "You are right. I am in love with her. But what if she doesn't love me? Then where am I?"

"You dummy!" Hjelmer said, patting him on the back so hard he nearly choked on the gust of air that blew out of his lungs. "It is as plain as the nose on jur face that she's loved ju from the day you got to Sawbill Landing."

"You really think so?" Byron asked. "Are you sure?"

"As sure as I am that Christmas is coming," Hjelmer said. "Now, vat's fer supper?"

"Coming right up," Helga said, making them aware that she had been listening to the whole conversation.

Good! Byron thought. *I could use a woman's perspective on this whole thing.*

After supper he would corner her and get some advice on how to handle a woman. Other than delivering babies and such, he didn't have a lot of experience with the weaker sex. *Ha! Weaker sex indeed!* He had never known anyone any stronger than Martha Tinker. Why, she could put any man to shame, the way she pitched right in at the logging camp. Yes, he might as well admit it; John Anderson was right—*he was in love.*

* * *

After a most enlightening conversation with Helga, Byron went upstairs to join Hjelmer. He was surprised to see Hjelmer lying on the floor, a quilt spread out underneath him.

"Why don't you sleep in the bed?" Byron asked. "I don't mind if we sleep together. I promise not to hog all the covers."

"Ju think I can fit in there?" Hjelmer asked, getting to his feet and lying down on the bed. His feet stuck through the iron bars on the foot of the bed so far they dangled from the knees down.

Byron laughed.

"It is either my feet or my head," Hjelmer said. "And my head is too big to fit between the bars."

The two men laughed together as Hjelmer returned to the makeshift bed on the floor. "No thanks, this is much better."

"So be it," Byron said, unfastening his boots and pulling them off. He turned the covers back and crawled into bed.

"Oofta!" Hjelmer said. "It's a far bigger yob to come to town than it is to chop down a whole forest full of trees." Before he could utter another word, he was sound asleep. Soon the room was filled with loud buzzing as he snored the night away.

Byron tossed and turned, covering his head with his pillow, trying to drown out the sound. Finally, he realized that it wasn't Hjelmer's snoring keeping him awake. No, it was far more than that. It was the dilemma he would face when he returned to Sawbill Landing. It was trying to figure out how to tell Martha that he was in love with her.

CHAPTER TWELVE

Long before sunrise, Hjelmer and Byron were up and dressed. They went downstairs to find Helga and John up as well.

"The sleigh is out back, and all of Miss Tinker's things are packed in it."

"I could have done that," Byron said, ashamed that he had put his host out with such a chore. He knew the bag was heavy; he had carried it upstairs for her that first night they had met, right here at this very spot.

"I'm sure you could," John said. "But now you don't have to."

"Thank you," Byron said, sniffing the air. "It smells wonderful!"

"Fresh baked bread," Helga said, "along with deer liver and eggs."

"Let's eat," Hjelmer said. They all knew that Hjelmer was *always* ready to eat.

As they ate, John and Helga joined them, like old friends.

"What's this about a beard from old Mrs. MacGregor's hair?" John asked.

Hjelmer cringed. "Isn't she the one they said yust died?"

"Lucky for me, she did," Byron said. "I was able to get some of her white bushy hair to have the barber make me a beard."

"Whatever for?" Helga asked. "You look mighty dapper without a beard."

"It's not for me," Byron said. "It's for Santa Claus."

"Santa Claus already has a beard," John said, conjuring up the image he had of the jolly old man.

"So I've heard," Byron said, then went on to explain. "The Koski kids out at the Landing, their father died before I got there. They are all alone for Christmas, them and their mother. She said they were crying one night because Santa Claus couldn't come out to the camp. He had never made it before, and surely this year, with their father gone, they just knew he wouldn't come."

"So you're going to be Santa Claus? And that's why you need the beard?" Helga said, clapping her hands in sheer glee. "How splendid of you!"

"Now you know why we have to get back to the camp right away. It would never do for Santa CLaus to be late for Christmas!"

"We have a little surprise for you," Helga said. "Seems Mr. Cartwright, over at the mercantile, figured out what you were up to after you bought the red long johns." She giggled at the image of Byron with the red underwear and white beard in place. "Well, you know, in a little town like Hibbing, news travels mighty fast. Before you could say 'jack rabbit', people were coming in here almost in a steady stream after you went to bed. The sleigh is all loaded with food for the people at the camp, warm clothes, quilts the women have made—all sorts of everything."

John disappeared out into the kitchen and soon came back with two chickens, their feet bound together so they could not get away. "They figured you didn't have any eggs, so this should give you at least a few."

"If somebody doesn't get hungry and eat the chickens," Helga teased.

"How can we take them back to camp?" Byron asked. "They'll freeze on the trip out there."

"Simple," Hjelmer said, picking one of them up by the neck. "Ve yust stick them inside our coats, like this," and he opened up his jacket and stuffed the bird inside. He laughed heartily as the hen tickled him. "Vell, ve might as vell get started. It's not getting any earlier."

"It sure isn't," Byron said, taking the other bird and sticking it inside his own jacket. It was going to be an interesting trip back to Sawbill Landing.

* * *

By the time morning arrived, Maya and Martha were back in their usual form. Whatever had hit them yesterday was a thing of the past. Today, just three days before Christmas, there was work to be done.

Martha had never cooked in her life, but Maya was unusually talented in that area. So, as Martha described the delicacies their family had always had at Christmas time, Maya made copies of the treats, using her creativity to find substitutes for the ingredients not found in the tiny logging camp. Soon the entire table was covered with tarts, pies, cookies, and even a fruit cake of sorts, using the wild berries she had dried in the fall.

It was mid-afternoon when they heard the sound of the horses returning. They ran to greet Byron and Hjelmer, and were surprised when they saw the sleigh, overflowing with presents from the people in Hibbing.

"What is all that?" Martha asked.

"That, my dear," Byron said, picking her up and twirling her around in the air, "is Christmas."

Martha saw her suitcase. She envisioned the garments she had so carefully packed, but which were no doubt crumpled after being left in the suitcase all these weeks. What would she do with them at Sawbill Landing? She looked down at her wool trousers and buffalo checked shirt and laughed. She felt far more at ease in them than she ever would in her fancy gowns again. *Still, you never know,* she thought. *There might be some occasion to dress up.*

"For Christmas!" she said, hit by inspiration. She looked at Maya and smiled. "For Christmas, you and I will be real ladies!"

Maya, not having the foggiest notion of what she meant, just smiled and nodded. "Real ladies," she repeated.

"We have to hide the sleigh until tonight, after the children have gone to bed," Byron said. "We want the gifts to be a surprise for them."

"Ve should take out the fruit, though," Hjelmer said, "or it vill freeze."

"Good thinking," Byron said, patting his friend on the back—well, at least above his belt line, which was as high as he could reach. "I'll go get them." He started to leave, but then turned back around, reached inside his jacket and pulled out the chicken, its legs still bound.

"What on earth?" Martha asked.

"There are two of them," Hjelmer said, pulling his hen out, too.

They had nearly smothered on the trip, but once they got a good dose of air into their lungs, they began to cackle like—well, like a couple of hens.

"They are, so we will have eggs," Byron said. "Amos Miller's sister sent them out. She said he always loved a good egg in the morning. So, now he can have one." He laughed, then added, "Provided, that is, that they cooperate and lay them."

"They vill," Hjelmer said, matter-of-factly. "They have to. They are Christmas chickens."

The two men disappeared, leaving Maya and Martha staring at each other. Then they broke into fits of laughter. "It's going to be a very good Christmas after all," Maya said.

"It is indeed," Martha said as she walked over to the table and picked up the rum-soaked cheesecloth the maple sugar had been wrapped in. "Mm, that smells good!"

"Merry Christmas, Uno," Maya said, taking the cloth from her and smelling it. "Thank you for your present."

* * *

Hjelmer and Byron pulled the sleigh out behind the long house where it was well hidden from view. It would be safe there for the next three days.

"So, are ju going to tell her?" Hjelmer asked.

"Tell who what?" Byron asked.

"Martha, of course," Hjelmer said. "Tell her that ju love her."

"I thought I would wait until Christmas," Byron answered. "You think that's okay?"

"Vatever ju think," Hjelmer said. "Yust don't vait too long."

Something in Hjelmer's tone made Byron ask, "Have you ever been in love, Hjelmer?"

"Once," Hjelmer said, "but there vas nothing I could do about it. She loved another man."

His answer made Byron pause. What if Martha turned him down? What if she didn't love him? What if…? Could he stay on at Sawbill Landing if they weren't together? They did make one terrific team, battling to save lives, fighting to improve conditions at the camp. When spring came, would she want to leave? He couldn't expect someone like her to devote her entire life to a place like this. His mind was whirling at a million miles an hour when he heard someone speak.

It wasn't Hjelmer's voice. It wasn't any of the men from the camp. In fact, as he looked around, he didn't see anyone. Yet he had heard it as loud and clear as if whoever it was had been standing right beside him.

"What did you say?" he asked, feeling foolish that he was talking to no one, or at the very least to himself.

"Trust in the Lord with all thy heart, and lean not to thine own understanding…"

"God?" Byron asked hesitantly. "Is that really you?"

"I shall give you the desires of your heart…"

And the only other thing he heard was the rush of the wind as it sang through the forest at Sawbill Landing. But he knew, deep within his heart, that Martha would say "Yes" when he asked her—on Christmas day—to marry him.

CHAPTER THIRTEEN

Christmas day dawned bright and crisp, the sun dancing off the snow glittering in its brilliance. Maya and Martha had worked hard to prepare a grand feast for the entire camp. The men began arriving early, all looking as eager as little children awaiting Santa Claus.

The Koski children, bouncing with excitement from the magic in the air, played and chattered busily. They had not had a real Christmas since they had arrived at Sawbill Landing. Their visions of Christmas were mainly from stories their parents had told them about life in the old country, but this year they huddled together, trying to imagine what it would be like if Christmas came—*really came*—to Sawbill Landing. They had lost their father; it seemed only right that someone or something should take his place, even if it was just for one day of the year.

The children usually had to wait until after the men finished eating, but today they were allowed to eat with them. No one mentioned the fact that Byron was missing. Maybe it was too much excitement in the air.

The men eagerly ate their oatmeal, knowing there would be a good meal later in the day. There was no work to be done today, other than for Maya and Martha. It was undoubtedly the busiest day they had spent in many years. But the looks of appreciation on the men's faces were payment enough for their labor.

Soon there was a rustling at the door, and a man, way too thin to be Santa Claus, but all dressed in *red long johns*, and a *very* bushy white beard, stumbled into the Koski shanty.

"Ho! Ho! Ho!" the man bellowed, trying to disguise his voice so the children wouldn't recognize him. "Santa Claus has gifts for all the little boys and girls at Sawbill Landing. How many do we have? One, two, three, four, five, six…"

"Don't forget me!" Hjelmer bellowed, sending them all into laughter.

One by one the men took the treasures they had made by hand and gave them to the children. They had agreed which men would give to which of the children so the gifts were evenly distributed. Santa Claus gave them candy and fruit, as well as small picture books and toys the people from Hibbing had sent out with them.

Martha had gotten her present from Byron early—the delivery of her suitcase. She had shown Maya the beautiful, hand-sewn designer gowns she brought from Boston. Today, on Christmas, both women were dressed in their finest and the men openly ogled them from time to time. It had been a long time since any of them had seen women. *Real* women, women who cried out to be recognized as women. But today there was no question about it; Maya Koski and Martha Tinker were two of the finest women on the planet.

Everyone had presented their gifts, except Hjelmer. Byron was tempted to ask him about it, but he didn't want to embarrass him. Finally one of the lumberjacks said, "Hey, Hjelmer! Don't tell me you didn't fix up a present for the Koski's. You told us you wanted to be left out of the drawing for children's names. Where's your Christmas spirit?"

Hjelmer blushed. He actually, truly blushed! Then he reached down and picked up the burlap bag that had been sitting by his feet. He handed it to Maya. "This is for all of ju," he said, with a shy smile. "I hope ju like it."

Maya opened the bag, then drew in a deep breath before she took the items out—one by one. First was the baby Jesus, all hand carved and tucked into his manger. Then she took out Mary and Joseph, the details on their faces making them seem almost alive. Next came the wise men, then the shepherds and even two little sheep. Finally came the angel, which seemed so real it was almost like she could hear the singing in the heavens as on that first Christmas day so long ago.

"They are beautiful!" Maya exclaimed as she set them in the middle of the table. Tears filled her eyes. "Did you...make them yourself?"

"I've been vorking on them for months," Hjelmer admitted. "It just seemed like ju needed them. And that was before Uno..."

The men all bowed their heads in respect of the men who had lost their lives during this terrible year. Suddenly, even with them gone, it seemed like everything was going to be all right again.

When everyone finished breakfast, Maya shooed them out of the kitchen so she and Martha could finish preparing the big meal, which they would eat in the late afternoon. With such a feast ahead of them, they had announced that there would be only one more meal this day. None of the men had complained. Several of them offered to help, but Maya insisted that this was "women's work." Now, alone in the kitchen, Maya admitted to Martha, "What I really meant was that they would be in the way more than they would help."

Martha laughed, knowing exactly what she meant. As they worked, singing Christmas carols and talking, they laughed about Byron and his Santa Claus outfit.

"Where did he get the beard?" Martha asked.

"I heard him tell one of the men that it was the hair off a dead woman!" Maya said. "Can you imagine?"

"And those red long johns," Martha said, laughing. "Did you see him scratching himself? They must have itched something awful!"

The two women were laughing when Byron stuck his head inside, now fully clothed in his normal garb. "Need any help?" he asked.

"You don't have anything we need," Maya said, winking at him.

"That's what you think!" he whispered as he turned and walked away. "We'll just see about that."

* * *

The men raved about the fine feast the women had prepared, with the help of the goods Byron had brought from Hibbing. By the time they were all finished the sun had already set, but in northern Minnesota that happened about four-thirty.

"I—we have one more present to show you," Hjelmer announced. "Martha, will you help me lead everyone to the tree?"

"If you will all go outside and wait for us to get our regular clothes on," Martha said. "I don't think either Maya or I would make it out there in this kind of a getup."

The men laughed. Soon Maya and Martha, dressed in their wool trousers, buffalo checkered shirts, heavy black wool coats, scarves and mittens, joined the men. Hjelmer instructed everyone to get their snowshoes and follow him and Martha.

As they tramped through the woods, the North Star lit their way, just as the men of old had been led. The newly fallen snow glistened in the moonlight. Byron stayed behind, walking with Maya. He watched Hjelmer and Martha, walking side by side, knowing they had made this trek before, probably alone. Jealousy roiled around inside him. What a fool he had been! He had asked Hjelmer if he had ever been in love with anyone. Of course! It all seemed so clear now. *Hjelmer was in love with Martha!* Was she in love with him, too? How could he think he stood a chance of winning her love?

"Trust in the Lord with all your heart..." It was that same voice. Was it mocking him? Or did he dare believe it? Would Martha say "yes" when he asked her to marry him? He had decided that tonight was the night. Now his knees nearly buckled. He had not felt such fear since the war. Perhaps this battle was as real as the one he had left behind.

Soon Hjelmer and Martha stopped. Hjelmer pointed up. The tree, which they had so carefully trimmed with natural things from the fields around them, was touched with God's own hand. Snow had fallen on the branches, making it complete.

"Look!" Martha exclaimed, looking up. "If you look just right, it looks like the Great North Star is sitting right on top of the tree!"

They all looked at it and marveled.

"It isn't dare," Hjelmer said.

Martha laughed as she pulled him down to his knees so he was even with the rest of them. "Now look," she said.

"Oh, my!" Hjelmer said excitedly. "It is dare!"

"Is there anything you'd like to do while you are on your knees?" one of the men yelled out at Hjelmer.

"Yeah, like pray?" another of the men chided.

"No," Hjelmer said. "I've prayed enough in the last few veeks to last a lifetime But there is one thing I'd like to do."

Byron froze. Martha was standing right beside him. Was this the moment he so dreaded? His heart was nearly leaping out of his chest, aching beyond human description.

"Maya?" Hjelmer called out.

Maya, surprised by his call, stood, frozen in her tracks.

"Don't make me go to ju," he said. "It's mighty hard for a man my size to get down on his knees, but it's even harder to get up. Come here."

It was a plea, not an order. Maya, looking completely shocked, walked to the spot where he knelt.

"Maya, before God and these people—our friends—I vant to ask ju if ju vud marry me." He hesitated. "I know ju loved jur Uno, but I have loved ju for a long time. But ju ver not mine. Ju belonged to another. But no more. Now ju are free. I vud not have vished Uno dead; he vas a fine man. But I vud like to take care of ju and the children. Please say yes. Or at least say ju'll tink about it. Maybe it's too soon, but..."

Maya looked at him. He was truly the most tender man she had ever known—other than Uno, of course. And she did owe it to the children to try to provide for them. She looked up, silently asking for some sign of approval from Uno. A shooting star blazed across the sky. Every one gasped, awed by such a sign of good will. Yes, she was fond of Hjelmer, and she could do a whole lot worse.

"Yes," she said, amid cheers all around them.

* * *

Byron felt like his sigh must have been so loud everyone in the group could hear it. *Maybe it was only Martha,* he thought as he realized that she had moved to stand beside him. Close enough to touch. Near enough to feel her breath on his face.

"Did you know?" Martha asked him.

"About Hjelmer and Maya?" he asked. She nodded. "I didn't have any idea," he said. "Did you?"

"No," she said. She wanted to reach up and feel his face. She wanted him to put his arms around her like he had when they rode on their single horse to Sawbill Landing that first day.

"It seems like love is in the air," he said, taking her hand in his and pulling her left mitten off. He reached into his pocket and took out the small gold band he had bought in Hibbing. It was the only thing he'd had to pay for; everything else had been given by the goodness of the people in town.

"I'm afraid that if I got down on my knees with snowshoes on, I'd never get up," he said, chuckling. "So just imagine that I am down there."

He looked deep into her eyes. "I know I am not Max Wilson. I know you came to marry him. But would you do me the honor of at least thinking about marrying me? I have loved you since the first day I laid eyes on you at the hotel in Hibbing."

Martha froze, not able to say anything. Byron's fears raced through his entire being. Had he made a complete fool of himself?

"Yes," she said softly.

"Yes, you will consider it?" he asked, knowing that was even more than he had dared to hope for.

"Yes, I will marry you," she replied.

The stars twinkled even brighter. The snow sparkled more than ever. God smiled down on them. It was Christmas! And Christmas was, after all, all about love. God's love to man. And if man just happened to fall in love on Christmas, what could be more perfect?

EPILOGUE

The years had passed and life had been good to the Fergusons. They had spent their lives at Sawbill Landing, and now they were much richer—nine children richer. Martha rested comfortably, their new son nestled in her arms.

"He's a good one," Byron said, reaching down and picking his newest son up. He rubbed his hand over the tiny heart, just as he had done with each new addition to the family. A wide grin spread across his face.

"This is the one," he said to Martha.

"How can you be so sure?" she asked, returning his smile.

"I can feel it here. He has a good heart. Yes, this one will be the doctor. He will devote his life to saving the lives of others."

"Just as you have done," she said, beaming proudly at her husband. His hair was now speckled with gray and his eyesight demanded the gold-rimmed spectacles he wore, but he was still as handsome as the first day she had laid eyes on him at the hotel in Hibbing. "You are a good man, Dr. Byron Ferguson."

"And you are the best wife any man could hope for," he said.

"You're sure?" she asked with a smile.

"Positive," he said, sounding even more sure of himself than before.

* * *

With Maya and Hjelmer Finseth at their side, the entire Ferguson family stood before the young minister who had come to start a church at Sawbill Landing. He reached over and took the tiny bundle in his arms and quoted some Scripture passages before he said, "I christen you Max Wilson Ferguson, in the name of the Father, the name of the Son and the name of the Holy Ghost."

The minister handed the baby back to Martha, who had a tiny tear in the corner of one eye. "You will make him proud of you," she whispered to her son. "Welcome to Sawbill Landing, Max." She smiled again. It was Christmas Eve. Yes, she reflected, even though it was scarcely a week since Max's birth, there was no question. She would don snowshoes and together, all eleven Fergusons, along with the rest of the people from Sawbill Landing, would make their way to *the* tree. She knew that Hjelmer had already been there to do the decorating. Yes, it was Christmas, and life was good.

"Merry Christmas, everyone!" Byron exclaimed as he walked through the forest with his family surrounding him.

"Merry Christmas!" they replied in unison.

...REVISITED

CHAPTER ONE

Martha Ferguson trudged home from school, tears trickling down her cheeks. It was almost Christmas. It was almost her birthday. She turned back and looked at the school in Hibbing, Minnesota. She usually loved to go to school, but any more she hated it.

It was 2002, and she had been told by her father and Grandfather Ferguson that she was a *special child.* She had heard the story over and over, but she loved it each and every time.

She was in first grade, and learning something new every day had been fun and exciting. But that was before…

She sat down on a rock, resting her elbows on her knees and tucking her chin into her hands. She was so lost in thought that she barely noticed her prized papers from school blow away. Big, fluffy white flakes tumbled down from the sky, but paid little attention to them either, nor that it was getting colder.

She wondered if she should go home. Maybe she could go to Grandfather Ferguson's. He was so wise; surely he would know what to do. Was it all her fault? She hated it when her mother and father fought, especially at Christmas time. It was supposed to be the season of peace and good will; her parents had taught her the true meaning of Christmas from the time she had been born. It had all seemed so right in the six short years of her life, and the fact that she was born on Christmas Eve had made it the perfect time of year. But that was those other years; this was this year, and nothing was right.

As the snow covered the hood on her red wool jacket, she thought about some of the other children in her class. Several of them had divorced parents. *What an ugly word,* she thought. She had never really understood it before, but now she was beginning to comprehend far more about it than she wanted to.

She had overheard her mother and father talking about it just last night. They'd been hollering at each other, then her mother had yelled, "Fine! If you don't like it, go ahead and *divorce* me." And then Martha heard the door slam shut and her mother was gone. *Gone!* And it was less than a week until Christmas. They were going to have a Christmas program at school. Would her mother even be there? Would they fight right in the middle of the play? And what about the Sunday School program? Surely they wouldn't fight in church!

"I don't know what to do!" she sobbed, sitting there now almost covered in the white snowflakes.

"'Tis the season to be jolly," a man's voice said as she felt a hand touch her on the shoulder. "What is the problem, little one?"

Martha looked up. She could hardly believe her eyes. There, right in front of her stood...*Santa Claus!*

"It's just awful!" she sputtered. "Everybody is supposed to be happy at Christmas, but I can't. Not this year. Maybe not ever again."

"There, there," Santa said, sitting down beside her on the big rock. "If you tell me all about it, maybe I can help."

Martha smiled through her tears. She wished the kids from school could see her now. Maybe it wouldn't matter if her mother didn't go to the school program. A wonderful idea hit her: *maybe Santa would go to her school play!*

"I—I need somebody to go to school with me," she said.

"Why?" Santa asked.

"Because I don't think my mommy will be there."

"Your mother is ill?" Santa asked, puzzled by the little girl's concern.

"No," Martha answered. "At least I don't think so. My mommy and daddy are gonna get a d—d..." She couldn't bring herself to say the word.

"They are going to get a what?" Santa asked.

"A...um...a...*divorce!*" There! She had said it. Like saying it out loud was going to make it happen, she began to cry harder.

"Are you sure?" Santa asked. "How do you know?"

"I heard them say so, just last night, after they had another big fight."

"Sometimes people, even grownups, say things they don't really mean," Santa said.

"But I know they did mean it," Martha said, "'cuz right afterwards Mommy left. And now when I go home, she won't be there. And Daddy will be working. I will be alone. And I don't even have a key to get into the house. And if I stay outside, I might freeze to death. And if they get a divorce, maybe Daddy won't come home either. And then what will I do? Oh, Santa!" Her voice pleaded for his help and understanding.

"Hold everything," Santa said, picking her up and setting her on his lap. "If we put our heads together, I'll just bet we can figure something out."

Martha tried her hardest to smile again. She wondered if the kids at school would believe her when she told them Santa himself had helped her. She thought about Timmy when he told about his pet turtle, and how it had saved the life of his lizard by getting in the way so the light didn't fall on it. Nobody had believed him. They probably wouldn't believe her, either. But it didn't matter.

Martha reached up and stroked Santa's fuzzy white beard. She had to make sure it was *really* him, not some phony just pretending. She'd seen some Santas like that. That's the only way there could be so many Santas in so many places at the same time. Satisfied that he was the real thing, she relaxed and cuddled against his big round belly.

"Now, for starters," Santa said, "why don't you tell me your name?"

"Martha," she said.

"Okay, Martha. Do you have a last name?"

"Ferguson," she replied.

Santa's eyes lit up with a twinkle. "You're Doc Ferguson's daughter?"

"Yes," she said. "At least I used to be."

Santa held her tightly. "I don't care if the whole world gets divorced," he said, "you will always be Doc Ferguson's little girl. Why, he loves you more than anything in the world."

"More than he loves my mommy, I know," Martha said sadly. "I guess that's good!" She climbed up on her knees on Santa's lap and kissed him. His whiskers tickled. She knew he really had to be Santa Claus; fake whiskers wouldn't tickle like that. It was Christmas, and if *anybody* could fix this whole mess, it had to be Santa Claus.

"Tell you what," Santa said, bouncing her up and down on his knee, "why don't we go over to your Grandpa Byron's house? Even if your mommy and daddy aren't home, I'm sure he would love to have you stop by for a visit." Santa laughed a hearty *Ho! Ho! Ho!* "In fact, I could use a cup of his good eggnog myself." He rubbed his stomach. "He makes the best in town, you know."

Martha looked quizzically at Santa. "How do you know that?"

"How do I know that?" Santa asked, letting loose with another round of *Ho! Ho! Ho!'s*. "Didn't your mommy and daddy ever tell you that Santa knows everything? He knows when you've been bad or good..."

"I've been good, Santa!" Martha nearly shouted. "Honest I have!"

"I know that," Santa said. "Don't you worry. I'll see that you get what you want for Christmas."

Martha wondered if he knew what she wanted for Christmas. No, not the toys she had put on the list for her mommy and daddy. What she *really* wanted. Or was it too much to ask for, even from Santa Claus?

Santa set Martha off his lap and stood up, taking her hand in his. Together they walked along the street, the snow falling. It looked like a perfect Christmas, even if it couldn't be.

After a few minutes they came to the street where her Grandpa Ferguson lived.

"Ready?" Santa asked, winking at her.

"Ready," she said. And together they went up to his apartment door and rang the bell.

CHAPTER TWO

"Martha!" Grandpa Ferguson said, surprised at seeing her. She always went directly home from school.

"Well, aren't you going to invite us in?" Santa Claus asked, winking at Grandpa. "It's getting a bit cold out there."

"It's always cold this time of year," Grandpa said. "Of course, I don't suppose it's nearly as cold in Hibbing as it is at the North Pole."

Good! Santa thought. *He's going to play along with me.*

"What brings you to this part of the world? Aren't you a little early?"

"Maybe," Santa said, shrugging, "but I sensed a little girl who needed me, so I decided to take a swing by to see if I could help."

"Martha?" Grandpa asked. "Are you in some kind of trouble?" He couldn't imagine what it might be. She was always a perfect child. He couldn't remember one time when she had needed correcting or punishment.

"No, Grandpa, not me," Martha said. "It's Mommy and Daddy. They've got *awful* trouble!"

"Max and Joan?" Grandpa asked. "Why, it can't be all that bad."

Santa motioned Grandpa off to the side and told him what Martha had confided in him. Grandpa scratched his head. He knew they were having some disagreements, but he never thought it would reach this point. He would have to have a talk with his son. But for now, he would see what he could do to put Martha at ease.

"You got any of that eggnog of yours?" Santa asked. "I sure could use a cup."

"Me, too," Martha said, a glimmer of enthusiasm beginning to shine. She loved her Grandpa Ferguson. It was beginning to look a lot more hopeful; between Santa Claus and Grandpa Ferguson, they could surely get this whole thing straightened out before Christmas. They had a whole week to work on it. That shouldn't be too hard—not for the likes of them.

As they sat drinking their eggnog, Grandpa began to tell stories about the first Dr. Ferguson who had come to Hibbing.

"Well, at least he stayed in town for one night," Grandpa said. "Then he headed out to Sawbill Landing."

Martha knew all about Sawbill Landing. Grandpa had told her about the logging camp many times.

"Grandpa, could you take me out to Sawbill Landing?" Martha asked. "You always said it was magic, especially at Christmas time."

"Not much left out there any more," Grandpa said. "Bunch of old run down tar paper shacks. Oh, except the house they built for my father. He was a doctor there, too, you know."

"And so were you," Martha said, "before you attired."

"Retired," Grandpa said, laughing. "But talking about *attire*, did I ever tell you about the time your great-great grandfather, the first Dr. Ferguson, played the part of Santa Claus at Sawbill Landing?"

Martha and the present Santa Claus had both heard all of his stories, but Grandpa Ferguson made it sound new every time.

"Tell us," Martha begged.

"Yeah," Santa said. "That's a good one."

And so Grandpa Ferguson told about Great-great-grandfather Ferguson's first Christmas at Sawbill Landing.

"And he ended up wearing the scratchiest red woolen underwear you ever saw, and his big white bushy beard was made from the hair the undertaker had cut off a dead woman."

Martha went over beside Santa and pulled on his beard again until he yelled "Ouch! Mine isn't from some dead woman; it's the real thing."

"Sorry," Martha said. "That won't count against me for what I want for Christmas, will it?"

"No," Santa said. "Say, you know, if I am going to get all the toys finished by Christmas, I'd better get a move on. You be okay here with your grandpa?"

"Fine," Martha said. It was funny, with Santa and her grandpa here, she had almost forgotten about all her problems. *Almost*, but not quite.

Grandpa walked Santa to the door, then stepped out into the hall with him.

"Think you can do anything about this?" Santa asked the senior Doc Ferguson.

"I'll get to work on it right away," Grandpa said. "If I need any help, can I count on you?"

"Of course," Santa, who Grandpa Ferguson knew as George Steiner, the long-time owner of the local hardware store, said.

Grandpa laughed.

"Something eatin' at your craw?" George asked.

"Nothing much," Grandpa said. "It's just that I believe you are the first Jewish Santa Claus I've ever seen in my life."

"Got a problem with that?" George asked.

"None at all," Grandpa said, laughing. "Makes perfect sense to me."

"Me, too," George said, then waved and disappeared into the elevator.

* * *

Grandpa took a cookie off the plate still sitting on the table, then turned back and got a second one. He went over and sat on the sofa, motioning for Martha to come and sit by him. He handed her one of the cookies and they each took a bite. Martha sighed—a sigh far too big to come from such a little girl.

"Want to start at the beginning?" Grandpa asked.

Martha looked up at him. She had those same big brown eyes his wife had. They could make you do anything in the world without saying a single word. If she asked him to leap tall buildings like Superman, he would go out and try it.

"Mommy and Daddy had another fight last night," she said, looking down, ashamed of confessing their private life to someone else. But this wasn't someone else; *this was her grandpa!* He had a right to know. He could help—him and Santa Claus.

"What were they fighting about?" Grandpa asked, hoping that if she could shed some light on the situation it might be easier for him to run interference.

"I'm not sure," Martha said, "but after a while Mommy told Daddy to divorce her. Then she left. And she hasn't come home since."

"Have you been home since you got out of school?" Grandpa asked.

Martha looked surprised. "No!" she said. "Do you think…"

"Why don't we go find out?" he suggested. "Wait while I grab my coat. I'm getting too old to be out in the cold." Soon he was beside her, and they headed down the stairs. There wasn't any point in waiting for the elevator; it was always too slow. They went out into the garage, climbed into Grandpa's four-wheel-drive jeep and headed for Dr. Max Ferguson's house—and, Grandpa prayed earnestly—to Martha's mother.

CHAPTER THREE

Grandpa knocked on the door. No one came, and he prayed once again that Joan would be there. It was Christmas, and she had no right to leave at a time like this. She had to consider what she was doing to Martha. And to Max. He deserved better than this. He had been born with that special Ferguson heart, the only one of their four children who had it.

From the time of the first Dr. Byron Ferguson's family on the Iron Range of northern Minnesota, each of the Ferguson families had had one special child. The first one had been Max, the youngest son of the original Byron and Martha. Legend had it that when each of their nine children had been born, Byron had placed his hand over their hearts; when it was Max's turn, Byron had known immediately that this child had the special gift. "The blessing," he called it. And Max had grown up to be a fine doctor, returning to Sawbill Landing to practice medicine after he completed his training.

Yes, Granpa knew all about *the blessing*. The youngest of Dr. Max's six children and named after his grandfather, he had received the gift. And he had lived with *the blessing* all of his life. There were times when he thought it was more of a curse than a blessing, for people always expected so much from him. But in the end he, too, had gone to medical school, then returned to become Sawbill Landing's doctor.

He had seen a lot of changes. Sawbill Landing had been the only logging camp in all of northern Minnesota that could boast their very own resident doctor. They had shown their appreciation by building a lovely wood house for him, complete with a fully equipped office. By the time he retired, which he didn't do until he was well up into his seventies, there wasn't much left of the logging camp. The last of the men moved out at the same time he left. Now there was nothing left.

Nothing but memories. And oh, how he loved to spin the tales of the bygone years at the logging camp. Nothing could ever equal it.

As he stood in front of his son's house, wishing life was as happy and simple as when he'd lived at Sawbill Landing, the door opened.

"Dad!" Joan said, surprised to see him. "Martha! I have been worried sick about you. Where have you been? When you didn't come home from school, I was so scared. *Where have you been?*" She raised her voice, more from fear than from anger. It was only three blocks from the school to their house, and Martha *always* came straight home. She was afraid she had been kidnapped, or hit by a car, or...

"I was with Santa Claus," Martha said. "He took me to Grandpa's. Then Grandpa brought me home."

"Santa Claus?" Joan asked. Her mind filled with the terrifying picture of some evil old man preying on children and doing God-knows-what to them while pretending to be the most wondrous friend a child ever had.

"I'll explain later," Grandpa said, trying to put her at ease. "She's been in good hands."

"Come on in," Joan said to her father-in-law. "Max will be home soon. I called him and told him Martha was missing."

"Who else did you call?" Grandpa asked.

"Just the school and the police," she said, "and the prayer chain from church."

"But you never thought to call me?" Grandpa asked, somewhat offended.

"Sorry," she said. "I wasn't thinking clearly."

"There seems to be a lot of that going around lately," he said, sounding far more accusing than he intended.

Joan wondered what Martha had told him. She didn't think Martha had heard the argument last night. She wondered what Max had told her this morning when she got up and found her mother missing. Did he make her out to be the villain? Maybe she was. She sure didn't feel like a hero. Not in this case.

She watched Martha as she sat with her grandpa, playing one of her favorite board games. She dialed each of the people she had called before, telling them that Martha was home and safe. Joan knew her father-in-law would stay until Max came home. She also knew that he wouldn't leave it alone. If he knew anything at all about the problems they were having, he would insist on getting to the bottom of it. He was more of a pain than a meddling mother-in-law ever thought of being.

"Joan!" Max hollered as he burst through the door. "Is Dad here? I saw his jeep out front."

"Hi, Daddy!" Martha said, running into his arms. "I'm so glad you came home. You and Mommy both! Maybe it's going to be a good Christmas after all!"

Martha's brown and white curly-haired, long-eared cocker spaniel loped into the room and rubbed up beside her legs. She reached down and petted her. "Hi, Scooter-Doo," she said. "Are you feeling better?"

"I still think we should take her in to see the vet," Grandpa said, leaning over to rub her behind the ears. Even that didn't seem to comfort her. "She just isn't like herself these days."

"I don't think that's necessary," Max said. "She's just getting a little fat and lazy."

"But you're not a vet," Grandpa insisted. "I still think…"

"Butt out, Dad!" Max said, surprising both himself and his father. He seldom spoke harshly to his father. In fact, he couldn't remember it happening before.

Must be the stress of the situation between him and Joan, Grandpa thought. Maybe tonight isn't the best time to get into it with them. Whatever it was, they were both here, together. Maybe they could find their way through whatever it was.

"Guess I'll be getting on home," Grandpa said. "Now that everybody is home safe and sound…"

"Thanks," Joan said, standing on her tiptoes to kiss him on the cheek. "I didn't mean…"

"I know," Grandpa said. "Don't worry about it."

"See you later," Max said.

"Thanks, Grandpa," Martha said, running to give him a big hug before he left. "Remember, you and Santa…" she whispered into his ear.

"I won't forget," Grandpa promised her. "And Santa won't either."

CHAPTER FOUR

Dr. Max, Joan, and Martha sat at the supper table, hardly a word being exchanged. Finally Joan asked Martha, "Tell me about this Santa Claus."

"He was real nice," Martha said, a smile appearing. "He took me to see Grandpa." She stopped, waiting for them to say something, but they both sat in silence, so she continued. "Grandpa knew him!"

Max laughed. "Of course Grandpa knew him," he said. "Grandpa knows just about everybody, and everyone knows Santa Claus!"

"No, not like that. I mean, Grandpa knew him. *And Santa knew Grandpa!*"

"How could you tell?" Max asked.

"He knew all about Grandpa's stories about Sawbill Landing." She paused a few moments, then asked. "Do you think Santa still goes to Sawbill Landing, just in case there's some kids there?"

"I wouldn't be at all surprised," Max said. "I'm sure Santa wouldn't forget any children."

"Does Santa *always* give boys and girls what they want for Christmas?" Martha asked.

"If he possibly can," Max said. "Sometimes—not often, but once in awhile—some children may ask for something that even Santa can't do."

"Like when kids are selfish and they want too many toys?" Martha asked.

"Exactly," Max said.

Joan sat and watched the interaction between her husband and her daughter. She loved her daughter, she really did. Yet she felt like an outsider. She knew that Max wanted another child more than anything else in the world. Was she being selfish by not letting him have what he wanted? She felt like a complete failure in the parenting department. She didn't want to risk causing more pain for another child. Maybe, if she worked at it harder, she could get closer to Martha.

It wasn't fair, she thought. To tell a little baby that they had inherited *the blessing* put far too much pressure on a child. It was an old family tradition, and she felt a tinge of jealousy. Her family never had any traditions. Not really. Not unless you could count going to the Country Club Christmas party a tradition. But that was so cold, so calculating, so *unChristmasy*.

Her mind wandered back to the first time she had met Max. They were both students at the University of Minnesota. He was in medical school, and she was in law school. They had met at a Christmas party on campus, and soon afterwards they began dating. They married the following year, exactly one week before Christmas. They had both finished their schooling, with Max going through his internship and her just starting in a law practice when he announced they were moving back to Hibbing.

That announcement had sparked their first argument. She didn't want to give up her new job, and he wouldn't budge either. It looked like they were locked in a stalemate, and she even considered divorce. But fate had thrown a monkey wrench into the whole mess when she discovered she was pregnant.

Max, of course, was thrilled. She, on the other hand, thought it was an *inconvenience*. She had never been close to her mother, and she found it hard to bond with her new daughter when she put in her appearance—on Christmas Eve.

"Damned Christmases anyway!" she grumbled, throwing her napkin onto her plate and storming off to their bedroom upstairs.

"What's wrong with Mommy?" Martha asked Max.

He wished he knew the answer. He knew he had been a bit too pushy about having another child lately, but he really didn't want Martha growing up as an only child. And he was sure Joan had grown to love Martha. She was just upset. Maybe it was hormones; God knows, in his medical practice he had seen more than his share of women who didn't make any sense at all.

"She's a little confused about some things," he said. "Give her time." He gathered Martha onto his lap and held her tightly. "She'll come around."

"You sure?" Martha asked, looking up at him with those big brown eyes that could melt icicles hanging from the roof, even in Hibbing, Minnesota.

"Positive," Max said, hoping she would believe him more than he believed himself. "Remember, it's Christmas. And miracles can happen at Christmas time, even today."

"Tell me about *the* tree," Martha said. She knew the story by heart; she had heard it every year. Sometimes even several times in one year. But she needed to hear it again, now.

Max told her about the very first Christmas tree Hjelmer Finseth and Martha's great-great grandmother, another Martha, had decorated. Each year the people at Sawbill Landing went back to the tree, and there were stories about real miracles that happened when they went to that tree on Christmas Eve. Miracles of love and life. Miracles that could not be explained by science or common sense. Miracles that only God could take credit for.

"I wish we could go to *the* tree," Martha said. "Maybe then Mommy could be happy."

Scooter-Doo rubbed up against her legs. "Even Scooter-Doo is sad this year," Martha said, and Max knew he couldn't argue with that.

Martha was correct; nothing was right this year. And the worst part of it was, he couldn't fix it. He could give in to Joan on the issue of more children, but it meant too much to him. He was the youngest of four siblings, and that was a pretty small family by Ferguson standards. He had been so close to his siblings as they grew up. Even now, he knew they would all be home for Christmas. *Especially* now. With Mom in the nursing home, they knew Dad needed them more than ever. Oh, why couldn't he just wave a magic wand and make everything like it used to be? He could work wonders at his office with his patients. Why was it so much harder when it was your own family—the people you love the most?

* * *

Dr. Byron Ferguson parked his jeep in the parking lot of the nursing home. He went inside, trying to sound cheerful when he greeted the receptionist and the nurses he passed on the way to his wife's room.

Elizabeth Ferguson, the sign on her door proclaimed. He pulled the paper out of the metal rim and crumpled it into a ball. How many times did he have to ask them to change that darned sign? She was *Bess!* She had been Bess all her life. No wonder she was confused; nobody had ever called her *Elizabeth.*

He walked into her room and immediately went over and pulled the curtains open. It was nearly sunset, but the bright red sun was still shining on the snow, and the room filled with warmth and light, as much from his presence as from the sunshine. He leaned over her and kissed her tenderly on the lips.

"Oh, Bess," he pleaded with her, "please come back to me. I need you."

It was not that long ago that it had happened, but it seemed like an eternity to him. Overnight she had become a stranger. He had taken her to the very best specialists in Minneapolis and even to the Mayo Clinic in Rochester, Minnesota. Their assessment was always the same: it resembles Alzheimer's, but it isn't clinical.

Not clinical! As a doctor, he had heard—no, he had *used* that term with his patients more times than he could count. If he were still practicing, he would never use it again, he was sure of that. It was so cold, so unfeeling. This wasn't some case study. *This was his wife!* The woman he had known and loved for over fifty years.

The final diagnosis was that she had suffered some traumatic event which had caused amnesia. It might be reversible, or she might stay that way for the rest of her life. Physically, she was in remarkably good health. But it wasn't safe to leave her alone, and Byron had finally agreed that it would be best for her to go to "the home."

But he had not given up on her. He spent hours every day sitting by her side, talking about things from their past, reading to her, watching television, eating together, or just sitting there holding her hand. And each day when he left he prayed for a miracle. He prayed for his Bess to return to him.

Today was no different. He stayed until nearly nine o'clock. It was his second visit today. He didn't have to go back in the evening. She probably didn't even know he was there. But after the mess at Max's house, he knew he had to be with her. He didn't belong anywhere else. If they had allowed it, he would have curled up in the chair and spent the night, but the nurse came in and announced, "Sorry, Doc Byron, but visiting hours are over."

As he walked out to the jeep, tears rolled down his cheeks. He looked up at the heavens, bright with stars in every corner, and wondered what was happening to his family. The Fergusons had always been strong; they were survivors. He wasn't about to give up now. It was Christmas, and miracles still happened, especially at Christmas time. He believed it with his whole heart.

CHAPTER FIVE

Martha lay in her bed, her head buried beneath her pillow. She wondered if even Santa could pull this one off. She had never seen her mother so sad. Even now, she could hear her crying in their bedroom. And she had heard Daddy tiptoe downstairs. She knew he was sleeping in the guest room. Would life ever be normal again? She finally fell asleep, her face stained with tears.

* * *

Joan sat on the edge of her bed, sobbing softly. She didn't want to keep Martha awake. None of this was her fault. She knew she wasn't being fair to her daughter, but she felt like such a failure. She got up and quietly walked to the closet and took a suitcase off the top shelf. She began to put her clothes into it, then went to the dresser and pulled the drawers open, taking her personal items out and putting them into the suitcase. She knew what she had to do. She had to leave, even if it was Christmas time.

As she picked up a scarf, something fell to the floor, making a *ping* sound. She bent over to see what it was. Her eyes welled with tears again. She sat back down on the bed, turning the item around and around in her hand, studying it carefully.

Her mother and father had been among the elite in Minneapolis, but her Grandmother Hays had always been her favorite. She was a "commoner," her mother said, but Grandmother Hays had more class than anyone Joan had ever known.

The tiny pin, which she had not looked at for years, offered her the comfort no one else could. The outside of the tiny circle was made from Grandma Hays' hair, carefully braided. Inside the circle was a picture of Grandma Hays.

"Please give me your strength," she pleaded. "I really need it—now more than ever before. I don't know what to do. I am so confused."

It seemed almost as if the face in the pin was talking to her. "Go see Grandma Ferguson," the voice said.

"That is crazy," Joan argued, even though there was no one there. "She doesn't even know who she is."

"Go see Grandma Ferguson," the voice said again. It was so real, Joan looked around to see if there was someone in the room with her. No, she was alone. Maybe she should be locked up with Grandma Ferguson! She was as loony as a cartoon.

She set the suitcase back inside the closet, half-packed, and crawled into bed. A calm came over her that lulled her to sleep almost immediately.

* * *

Max sat in the recliner in the living room. There was no point in trying to get any sleep. He knew it wouldn't come. Not tonight. Not until he figured out what was wrong with his wife. He had fallen in love with her, and they had been so happy. And when Martha was born, she had seemed to overcome the fears she had about having a child. He knew she loved Martha. *How could she ignore her now?* Their daughter needed her. She needed both of her parents. For God's sake, *it's Christmas!*

His mind wandered back to the tales his father had spun about life at Sawbill Landing. He had lived there as a child, but the camp had eventually broken up, and the logging industry had taken its toll on the camp, like it did one after another in northern Minnesota. The logging industry had become one of huge trucks and tractors, not men with saws and horses.

Off in the distance, he heard a voice, like the wind whispering through the pines in the camp. "Go see your mother."

Max snapped the chair into an upright position and jerked his head around. Who was that? He thought he was alone. Was it his father? Had he come back to see what was really going on? He knew Dad wouldn't leave it alone until he got to the bottom of the problem. Dad was just that way; he never let anything rest until it had a solution.

The room was dark, and he could not hear anyone there. Was he losing his mind? The stress had been hard on him, but he had to get control of himself. He lay back in the chair and tried to get to sleep. His mind played his life over and over, like a continuous tape on a VCR. He saw their wedding, their first apartment, *the* tree, Martha's birth, the day his mother had to go to the nursing home, *the* tree, the day his father retired and they moved into Hibbing, *the* tree, his first job, his college days, *the* tree...

Did *the* tree hold the secret to their future happiness? He had never really believed in the magic of that big old tree out in the middle of the forest at Sawbill Landing. It was a fable, a myth. If it made his mother and father feel better, he didn't want to ruin it for them. But he was wiser than them, part of a new generation. He had always needed proof of how things worked, had always found a logical explanation for whatever happened. There wasn't any logic in some silly old pine tree. That was as far-fetched as believing in Paul Bunyan.

He didn't know what convinced him of it, but somehow he decided—whether he was asleep or awake he didn't know—that he had to get to *the* tree on Christmas Eve. That was when the magic was supposed to happen.

By the time daylight came, every single member of the Ferguson family had a new sense of purpose for the holiday season. Christmas was all about love, all about family. No one knew exactly how they were going to manage it, but somehow they would all be together for Christmas. This year and every Christmas to come.

* * *

Martha got up and dressed herself for school in a warm, fuzzy jogging suit. She went downstairs and was surprised to find her father still there.

"Daddy," she said, running to him and giving him a big hug. "Why are you still home?" Her face was suddenly filled with terror. "Did something happen to Mommy?"

"No," he said, hugging her back. "She's very tired, so I thought I would let her sleep in." The radio played Christmas music in the background. "It's pretty cold out this morning," he said. "I'll drive you to school."

"I can walk, Daddy," she said. "I'll be okay. It isn't that far." She didn't add that she really hoped she would see Santa again. She needed to have what Grandma had always called a *confab*. If they were going to get this thing all worked out in less than one week, they had to get their plan figured out. This was going to take some big time figuring, but she was up to the job. She and Santa and Grandpa. No, sir, there was no task too big for the three of them.

CHAPTER SIX

Her father had insisted on driving her to school, so Martha watched both sides of the streets as they drove, hoping to catch a glimpse of Santa Claus. She was disappointed when they pulled up at the school; there had been no sign of him.

Jamie, her best friend, came running up to the car to greet her.

"Hi!" she said cheerily. "What's the matter?"

"Nothing," Martha said, hoping her friend would believe her. Still, if Jamie insisted on knowing, Martha knew she could tell her. She could tell Jamie just about everything.

The two girls walked into the school together. Max drove away slowly, knowing it wasn't fair for such a little girl to have to bear the burden of the problems between him and Joan. He had to figure out some way to get past them. *The* tree! The image of the huge old pine out in the middle of the forest seemed to stand right in the middle of the road. Before he realized what he was doing, he discovered that he was in front of the nursing home where his mother was.

He found a parking spot and pulled up the hood on his parka. The wind was howling, and the air was icy. He ignored the receptionist as she said, "Merry Christmas, Dr. Max." He was on a preprogrammed route to his mother's room. He didn't have any control over his actions. He had never felt like this before. He was a doctor, with a scientific mind; his life didn't function this way, but there was nothing he could do about it.

"Good morning, Mother," he said as he kissed her on the cheek. He sat down on the edge of the bed facing her in her rocking chair.

"Mother," he said, "I don't know what to do. And I sure don't know what you can do. I don't even know if you know who I am. Mother, everything in my life is so mixed up. Joan and I are fighting, and Martha thinks she is to blame for it, and Dad can't think about anything except you, and Dad and Martha insist they had eggnog and cookies at your apartment last night with Santa Claus. Mother, I mean, they think he was the *real* Santa Claus."

His mother sat there, staring straight ahead, her eyes glazed over. If she heard one word of what he said, she gave no sign. Not to him. Not to anyone.

It didn't matter to Max. He had to talk to someone. Whether or not they were able to comprehend any of it, at least he felt better having voiced his frustrations.

"It's all about children," he continued. "I couldn't imagine growing up without any brothers and sisters. I want desperately to give Martha that, but Joan can't face the thought of having another baby." He continued, taking a quick gulp for enough air to keep going. "She is being so selfish, Mother, and it isn't fair. Not to me, or to Martha. She didn't want a baby when Martha was born either, but she loves her. I know she does. She just doesn't know how to show it. I know if she had another child, she would love it, too."

He knelt down in front of her, taking her fragile, shaky hands in his. "Oh, Mother, please...*please* tell me what to do!"

He waited, not expecting an answer. His eyes snapped open wide when he heard her voice.

"*The* tree," she said.

Max shook his head. Had he imagined that she had spoken? Why, after all this time, would she be concerned about *the* tree? Of course he didn't have to ask her which tree she meant. Their entire family knew the history of *the* tree. The Germans might have their *tannenbaum,* the English their Yule log, but the Fergusons and everyone who had ever lived at Sawbill Landing had their tree. It was simply called *the* tree; it didn't need any more of a description that that. Oh, yes, Max knew all too well what she meant.

Maybe he had thought about it so much in the last few hours that he imagined she said it. He could always put her to the test. If she repeated it, he would have to take her seriously. But he knew better than to expect her to say something twice. Once was a miracle.

A miracle! Isn't that what she had always taught him Christmas was all about? Why shouldn't there be some miracles for Christmas this year? If there was ever a year that he needed a miracle, this was it. Hesitantly, he asked, "What did you say, Mother?"

As naturally as if she had never stopped talking, she repeated, "*The* tree."

Max shook his head. This time he had been expecting it. Well, at least more than the last time. No, there was no question about it; she had spoken.

Max, still kneeling in front of her like he had done when he was a little boy, looked up at her. Her eyes were still glassy, but his were filled with tears.

"Oh, Mother! I don't understand any of this, but if you say I should go to *the* tree, I will go to *the* tree." He took a tissue from the box on her bedside table and wiped his eyes. "Should I go alone? Or should I take Joan and Martha with me? Or should I wait until the other kids come? Maybe we could all go together." He jumped up and hugged his mother. He wasn't sure, but he thought he saw her smile! It had been so long since he'd seen the corners of her dainty mouth turn upward. If this was the only miracle he got for Christmas, it would have to do. Was it possible? Would his mother come back to them? *Could* she come back?

* * *

When the lunch bell rang, Jamie hurried over to Martha.

"You can tell me nothing is wrong, but I don't believe you," she said. "You didn't even hear it when Mrs. Peterson called on you—*three times!* I know something is wrong. If you don't tell me—*I won't be your friend anymore!*" She put her hands on her hips and started to walk away.

"Wait!" Martha said, trying as hard as she could not to cry. "I'll tell you, but you have to promise not to tell anyone else."

"Promise," she said, raising two fingers in their secret code. "Now, spill it!"

Martha hung her head, like she was ashamed of her own life. "Mommy ran away from home."

"That's impossible!" Jamie said, so loud that Martha slapped her hand over her friend's mouth so everybody in the lunchroom wouldn't hear her. Much more quietly, she said, "Mommies can't run away from home. That's only for kids to do."

Martha remembered the time Jamie had gotten mad at her parents about something—she couldn't remember what it was about, now—she had run away from home. She took a little tent and set it up the best she could in the back yard—out behind the garage so they couldn't see it. She was fine until it got dark and a cat started meowing. Then she high-tailed it into the house as fast as her little legs could carry her. Remembering that made Martha laugh. She wondered if her mother had set up a tent behind their garage, too. If she did, she didn't get scared. Or had she? She had come back home.

"But I think it's going to be okay," Martha said. "It has to be!"

"How do you know?" Jamie asked.

"Santa promised me," Martha said matter-of-factly. "Santa doesn't lie!"

"Santa?" Jamie asked. "How do you know that?"

"Because he said so, last night when I talked to him."

Jamie's big eyes rolled in disbelief. "You talked to Santa last night? Where? And how? Don't tell me you've got his telephone number."

"No, silly," Martha asked. "Nobody knows Santa's number, except maybe Mrs. Claus. And maybe some of the elves."

Jamie scratched her head. "Santa is only at the department store on Saturday," she said. "Yesterday was Tuesday."

"I know," Martha said. "I was sitting on a rock. You know, that big one on the way home. I was trying to figure out why Mommy and Daddy were fighting so much. I think maybe it's my fault." She looked sad. "I don't think Mommy likes me very much."

"Martha!" Jamie said, almost shouting again. Martha's expression made her lower her voice. "I'm sorry, but that's an awful thing to say. Everybody's mother has to like them. I think it's a law or something."

"But she acts so, I don't know, mad or sad or upset, when we're alone together."

"I don't think that's it," Jamie said. "I think maybe your dad did something that made her mad. I know that happens at our house sometimes, but it always goes away. I'm sure in a couple of days it will be all over and everything will be like it's always been."

Suddenly, as though she had seen a big sign in the sky, Martha said, "Santa took me to Grandpa's. Grandpa told us the story about *the* tree. Have you ever heard that story?"

Jamie looked confused. "What tree?" she asked. "A Christmas tree?"

"Not just *any* Christmas tree. It's *the* Christmas tree. It's out in the forest by the logging camp where my daddy grew up. It's a magic Christmas tree. Grandpa says miracles happen by *the* tree on Christmas Eve. If I could just get Mommy and Daddy to go out there on Christmas Eve, I know everything would be okay."

"I never heard of a magic Christmas tree," Jamie said.

"Can you come over to Grandpa's with me after school?" Martha asked. "If *Grandpa* tells it, I know he'll make a believer out of you, too."

"I'll have to call my mom and ask her if it's okay," Jamie said. "I like your grandpa's stories."

"This is his very best one," Martha said. "You'll just love it."

* * *

Byron walked into the nursing home, his gaze firmly fixed on the floor, his footsteps long and determined. He headed directly for his wife's room.

"What's gotten into him?" one of the nurses asked a fellow-worker.

"Beats me," the other one answered. "He must have watched too much Scrooge on TV last night."

"Yeah," the first nurse said, "but that's not like Doc Byron. He's always got a friendly word."

"Not today. Think we should follow him and try to find out? I hate to see him so down. He's been such a trooper with his poor wife here and all."

"What?" the nurse asked, placing her hand on her heart. "And spy on the good doctor? Why, I never!" Then she swung around on her heel and headed in the same direction Dr. Byron had just gone. "Who will know?"

The other nurse grinned—it was fun getting in on somebody else's business. Her friend was right; who would know?

Dr. Byron harrumphed as he glared at the sign on the door. "Elizabeth!" he sputtered. "Why can't anybody ever get things straight?" He pulled it out again, as he had done on every visit, but this time it was with more force than usual.

Inside the room, he was surprised to find Bess sitting in the chair, looking out the window. It was the first time he had seen her do that since she had come. Usually she was in bed.

Was this a good sign? Was "Santa" right? George had stopped by for coffee this morning and had insisted that things in the Ferguson family weren't as bleak as they seemed. "It is still the season of miracles," he'd said.

Odd, Byron thought. *It takes a Jew to make me remember what Christmas is all about.* He had delivered more than his share of babies over the years, and each one was a new and wonderful miracle. He smiled again as he said, without noticing that he was speaking out loud, "Of course. The baby Jesus was a Jew, too."

"Good afternoon, darling," he said to Bess. He kissed her tenderly. He felt his heart race when she kissed him back. Was it possible? Was she coming back to him? He had almost given up hope, but his faith and expectancy were suddenly renewed. He began to talk to her, realizing he was waiting for her to answer him.

"Has Martha been here to see you?" he asked. His face fell, along with his hope, when there was no response. No look of recognition on her face. Nothing. It was just the same as every other day. Maybe the kiss was just his imagination playing tricks on her.

"Sweetheart, we've got trouble brewing. I know, somehow, that you can hear me. I don't expect you to help me out on this one. I just want you to listen."

He paused, waiting for a reaction from her. Nothing. But he continued anyway. "You know there has never been a divorce in the Ferguson family. Well, I'm not going to allow for one now. Not if I can help it."

He sat down on the bed, facing her, and took both of her hands in his. "Max and Joan are having problems. I don't know the full story. Max wouldn't discuss it with me. I found out from Martha. George Steiner found her sitting on a rock out in the snow yesterday, so he brought her over to the apartment. She was so upset. Seems Joan walked out on them last night, leaving the poor child scared to death."

He looked at her and he could swear he saw one tiny tear in her eye. Did she really understand him? Had she heard and understood everything he had told her all these months? He ran his hand softly over her cheek. "Oh, Bess, I love you! I wish you could just tell me what to do."

"Go to *the* tree," she said, so softly he wasn't sure he hadn't imagined it. She had not said a single word in so long.

"Oh, Bess!" he said, his voice filled with love. "Tell me more. Please!" But nothing more came. That was it. Just "Go to *the* tree."

He knew he couldn't argue with her. Yes, he would find some way to get the whole family back to Sawbill Landing. Back to *the* tree. "I will take you, too," he promised, embracing her warmly. He smiled, then said, "I hate to leave you, but I've got to start making plans."

He walked out, pausing at the doorway to turn back to smile at her. Yes, it was going to be a good Christmas after all. A *very* good Christmas.

* * *

Joan parked the car. She spotted Dr. Byron's jeep in the parking lot, so she left the engine running until he was gone. She angrily flipped the radio off when it began to play "Happy Holidays." She didn't feel happy, so why did they have to insist on rubbing it in?

It was, she now conceded, all her fault. Maybe another baby wouldn't be so bad. She wasn't about to go back to her law practice, anyway. Max provided a very good living for them—far more than comfortable. There was no question about them having enough money for one more mouth to feed.

But it was more than that. It was all about her and her own inadequacies. It was not fair to bring another child into the world if you didn't have enough love to offer them.

Suddenly, the radio turned on again. She knew she had turned it off, but here it was again. She tried to turn it off, but the song continued. There must be a short in it, she thought. She'd take it to the garage in the morning. She didn't need somebody spewing forth wishes of peace and good will.

She listened to the song they were playing. It was a melancholy song about a little boy who Santa forgot. The ending revealed the boy's daddy had left him.

Her thoughts shifted at once to Martha. Was she as cruel to her daughter as that daddy was to his little boy? She was flooded with feelings of guilt, then of regret. She closed her eyes, trying to block everything out of her mind. As though in a trance, she pictured Martha in a few years, sitting alone in front of a huge Christmas tree. She looked around to see if somebody was in the distance, but no, Martha was definitely alone. The radio played "Blue Christmas," then turned off.

Joan snapped back to reality and looked up; Byron's jeep was gone. She pulled the key out of the ignition and headed inside. Like Byron just a little earlier, she didn't stop to talk to anyone, but went straight to Bess's room.

"Hi, Mom," she said, trying to sound cheerful. "What's happening?" She smiled, in spite of how she felt. Did she really think Bess was going to answer her? Who was she trying to kid? Her mother-in-law hadn't spoken in ages; what made her think she would start now? That would take a miracle.

"Dad was just here," Bess answered, like it was perfectly normal.

Joan jumped. "Mom, did you say something?"

"Dad was just here," she repeated. "He says you are getting a divorce."

Joan's face went white. She hadn't intended Byron to know about that, and she certainly never meant for Bess to find out. She had problems far more serious to worry about than the mess Joan had made of her marriage to Max.

Joan began to tell Bess that it was just something they had to work out, and that she shouldn't worry about it. "You know how everything always gets exaggerated," she said. She forced a laugh, but it sounded hollow, even to her.

She waited for Bess to say something else, but silence filled the room, just like always.

"Mom," she said, "I know you can help me." Then she began to pour her heart out to the woman who had always been so wise, but who seemed now to be just a shell of someone she used to know. Although she hadn't intended to, Joan told Bess the whole story—how she felt like such a failure, how she had never learned to love, how she had failed Martha, how she didn't deserve to be a part of such a wonderful family...

Joan took Bess's hands in hers, just as Byron had done such a short time ago, and just as Max had done earlier in the day. "Oh, Mom," she said, "I don't understand it, but I just feel like somehow you are the one who holds the key to getting this whole mess straightened out. Tell me, what should I do?"

"Go to *the* tree," Bess said, then withdrew inside her shell again, just like a turtle trying to protect itself from outside forces.

Joan tried to get Bess to say something else, but it was a lost cause. Eventually she gave up and went out to her car. She started it, then switched on the radio. It was dead. No matter what she did, it was silent. She had to get it checked out in the morning. She did like a radio to keep her company—at least under usual circumstances. She wondered if anything this year would be normal.

CHAPTER SEVEN

Martha and Jamie went up to Grandpa's apartment and rang the bell. When no one answered, Martha turned the knob and walked in; Jamie stayed behind in the hallway.

"Aren't you coming in?" Martha asked.

"Nobody's home," Jamie said, confused.

"He'll be back before long," Martha said confidently. "Besides, Grandpa never locks his door because he says somebody might need a place to stay."

Jamie cautiously entered, looked around, and smiled as she walked over to the tabletop pinecone Christmas tree. Martha flipped the switch on the cord on, making the tiny lights dance.

"That's beautiful!" Jamie said. "I've never seen anything like it."

"Grandma made it before…" Martha's face turned serious, then glowed with excitement. "Let's take it over to Grandma!" she said. "Maybe it will make her feel like Christmas! She always *loved* Christmas."

"But wouldn't your grandpa miss it?" Jamie asked, not at all sure that they should take it without permission.

"Okay," Martha agreed, "we'll wait until Grandpa comes home, but then we'll ask him if we can."

The door creaked as it opened and Grandpa came in, his arms loaded down with so many packages he could hardly see over the top of them. "Somebody here?" he asked.

"Surprise!" Martha shouted gleefully.

Grandpa set his packages down, then went to Martha and gave her a big hug. "This is the nicest surprise I've had in…let's see…" He grinned at the girls. "…since you came over yesterday."

"I like your tree," Jamie said, pointing at the pinecone tree.

"We were wondering if we could take it over to Grandma," Martha said. "What do you think?"

"I think that's a wonderful idea," Grandpa said, grinning widely at them. "She always loved Christmas."

"I told Jamie that, didn't I, Jamie?" Martha asked, and Jamie nodded.

"Can we take it now?" Martha asked, just as Jamie nudged her with her elbow and reminded her "You were going to have him tell me about the tree."

"It's not the tree," Martha said. "It's *the* tree!"

"Sorry," Jamie said. "I didn't know."

Grandpa sat down on the sofa and motioned for the girls to join him. When one was on each side of him, he began to tell the story of *the* tree—the very first time it was decorated at Sawbill Landing by Martha Ferguson and Hjelmer Finseth.

"She was my great-great grandmother, wasn't she, Grandpa?"

"She sure was," Grandpa agreed. "You were named after her."

"I'm *special!*" Martha said, puffing her chest out proudly.

"My mom says *I'm* special, too," Jamie said, shrugging.

"But my daddy could feel it in my heart," Martha said, trying to explain. "Before this, it's always been one of the boys who was *special*. But when I was born and Daddy put his hand on my heart, he could feel that I was the special one."

Jamie began to get a little aggravated at Martha's bragging. "Of course you were the special one," Jamie, who had three brothers and two sisters, said. "You are the *only* one."

"I know I am," Martha said, suddenly breaking into tears. "You don't know how awful that is." She went to her very best friend and hugged her. "I'm so glad I at least have you." She wiped her tears on her mittens. "I prayed real hard that Santa would give me a brother or sister for Christmas. But I know it's not going to happen. Not now. Not ever. Mommy doesn't even want me; she sure won't want any more babies."

"What on earth gave you that idea?" Grandpa asked, studying her reaction closely.

"I heard them fighting the other night," Martha said. "That's what they were fighting about. Daddy said he wants another baby, but Mommy says no. She was really mad about it. Then she ran away from home."

Oh, my! Grandpa thought. *The things a grandfather has to do. I guess I'd better go have a talk with...* No, it wouldn't do any good to talk to Max; he had the right idea. He would have to go confront Joan. Would she think he was a meddling old fool? She might be right. Still, he needed to set his daughter-in-law straight. No family deserved to have only one child. There was no better time; Christmas was all about the birth of a very special baby.

"You said you want to take the little tree over to Grandma? I'll drive you over there," Grandpa said.

"No, we can walk," Martha insisted. She couldn't explain why, but she felt that she needed to talk to her grandmother alone. She would have to get Jamie to wait outside Grandma's room, at least for a few minutes. Then she could come in, too. Maybe it would help Grandma to see children. She had always seemed more like a child than an old lady to Martha, anyway. They had always understood each other, even when no words were exchanged. Maybe, just maybe, there would be a way to get past the problems they had all had, especially at Christmas time.

***

"Hi, Grandma!" Martha said. "Look what I brought you." She set the little pinecone Christmas tree on the dresser and hunted around until she found an outlet to plug it into. The little lights twinkled warmly. "See, Grandma? It's just like *the* tree, only littler."

Grandma *laughed!* Martha jumped. Grandma hadn't laughed in so long... She ran to her grandmother and threw her arms around her neck. "Oh, Grandma!" she exclaimed. "I knew something good was going to happen. It's Christmas, Grandma! Did you know that?"

Grandma did not answer Martha, but the way her eyes lit up, Martha was sure she understood. Everybody thought Grandma didn't know what they were talking about, but maybe they were wrong. Maybe she was just trying to fool everyone so she could find out what was *really* happening. Martha had the strange feeling that everyone in the family confided in Grandma but never told anyone else they did, and Grandma never let on that the others had been there.

Grandma laughed—again! Twice in one day! Martha took her hands in hers, rubbing them gently. "Did you hear what I was thinking?" she asked, even though that didn't seem to make any sense at all.

Grandma laughed—a third time! She wriggled her finger for Martha to come close to her.

"Can you keep a secret?" she asked Martha, her voice little more than a whisper.

"You bet!" Martha said, wanting to jump up and down. Grandma was actually talking to her!

"Everybody thinks I'm crazy," Grandma said.

"Are you?" Martha asked.

Grandma smiled.

"I don't think so," Grandma said honestly. "I don't know what happened to me. All of a sudden I couldn't remember anything. It was so scary. I knew all of you when you visited me, but I couldn't remember how to talk!"

Her eyes filled with tears as she relived the terror of realizing she'd forgotten how to speak. "I tried. Oh, I tried so hard, but I couldn't get the words out. Then people would tell me about things that had happened, and I didn't know what they were talking about."

Grandma paused, pulling Martha down onto her lap. "I was afraid nobody would come to see me, because they thought I didn't know if they were here or not." A tear trickled down her cheek. "But you all kept coming. You all loved me! Most of all, Grandpa kept coming. Every day. Sometimes even two or three times a day. Oh, how he must have hated it!"

"Grandpa never hated coming to see you," Martha said. "He was just so sad because of how you were."

"How do you know that? Did he tell you?"

"He didn't have to," Martha said. "I could see it in his eyes." She snuggled closer to her grandma. "He loves you."

"What do you know about love?" Grandma asked.

"I know Daddy loves me," Martha said, "and Mommy doesn't."

Grandma was shocked. Did Martha know all about the troubles her parents were having? It wasn't fair to make a little girl carry that kind of a burden. She would have to see what she could do about it. If she could just plant the seed, again and again, that she had set in place today…

"Of course your mother loves you," Grandma said. "What makes you think she doesn't?"

"I heard her and Daddy fighting," Martha confessed. "I was supposed to be asleep, but they were hollering *so loud*. Mommy told Daddy, *You know I have never liked children*."

"She didn't mean you, darling," Grandma said.

"But she said…" Martha said, trying hard not to cry. She'd come here to cheer Grandma up, not to talk about her parents' troubles, but before she could stop herself she had spilled the whole story, right down to the fact that they planned to get a divorce.

"They will do no such thing!" Grandma said, stomping her foot so hard Martha nearly fell off her lap. "No Ferguson has ever had a divorce, and your father is not about to be the first one!"

"But how can you stop them?" Martha asked. Everyone in the family used to listen to Grandma's advice. But now, they didn't even know she could talk. Or remember. Or figure anything out.

"You have to trust me," Grandma said. "And I need your help."

"I'll do *anything!*" Martha said, thrilled with the idea that she and Grandma could make this whole nasty, ugly divorce business go away. "Just tell me what to do."

"It was such a funny day today," Grandma said, smiling. "One by one they all showed up here. Your daddy told me he and Joan were having trouble, and that it was all about having more babies." Grandma shivered. "Such nonsense! Having babies is the most natural thing in the world. Grandpa was all mixed up by the whole thing, and he didn't know what to do to help. And your mother, well, she is feeling so guilty. Then you come along, and at last I have somebody I can talk sense with."

"They all came to see you today?" Martha asked, surprised. "What did you tell them?"

"I didn't let them know I remember things now," Grandma said. "You can't tell them, either."

"I promise," Martha said, pretending to lock her lips and throw the key over her shoulder. "My lips are locked."

"Good girl," Grandma said. "I only told them one thing."

"You talked to them?" Martha asked.

"I only said one thing," Grandma admitted. "I told each of them to go to *the* tree."

"Why?" Martha asked.

"Hasn't Grandpa told you the story of *the* tree?" Grandma asked.

"Of course," Martha said. "In fact, he told Jamie the story just this afternoon."

"Jamie?" Grandma asked.

"Oh, yes," Martha said. "Jamie is my very best friend." She opened her eyes wide. "Oh, my goodness! I left her out in the hall waiting for me!"

Martha ran to the door and opened it, looking up and down the hallway. She smiled when she spotted her friend, sitting with an old man and talking, both of them laughing. She came back inside, shut the door and sat down on the bed, facing Grandma.

"But I still don't understand why you told everybody to go to *the* tree," Martha said.

"If Grandpa has told you the story, surely you know that on Christmas Eve it is magic. Miracles have happened at that tree for years. Every Ferguson has at least one tale to tell of the miracles that have happened to them when they stood by *the* tree on Christmas Eve."

"What was *your* miracle?" Martha asked.

"Your daddy," Grandma replied. "When he was four years old, he climbed a tree. *Way* up. He had done that lots of times, but this time he fell. Uncle Bill carried him home, and by the time they got to the house, they were both covered in blood. We were so afraid we were going to lose him." Once more, the tears ran down her cheeks. "He was unconscious for over three weeks. We didn't think he would ever wake up."

"But he did," Martha said. "He's okay now."

"On Christmas Eve, we put him in the old red wood sled, all tucked in with quilts. It was so cold! I didn't think we should take him, but Grandpa insisted." She chuckled. "I wasn't really sure about *the* tree. I wasn't born a Ferguson, you know; I married into the family. It takes longer for us to believe."

"So what happened?" Martha asked, spellbound by Grandma's story.

"At exactly midnight, we were all standing there, dozens of us, circling the tree, holding hands. All of a sudden Max looked up and said 'Merry Christmas!' like nothing had ever been wrong."

"Was it magic?" Martha asked.

"Call it what you want to: magic, miracles, God. It didn't really matter to me what it was. All I knew was that I had my little boy back and everything was all right with the world." She looked at Martha. "And then it happened."

"Something else happened?" Martha asked. "What?"

"The star," Grandma said, beaming as brightly as the Star of the East in Bethlehem on that first Christmas night so long ago.

"What about the star?" Martha asked.

"Whenever there was a miracle at *the* tree, a bright star would appear in the perfect place so when you looked up it was just like it was sitting on top of *the* tree. Most times it could only be seen by the people who received the miracle, but sometimes, on very special times, *everybody* could see the star."

"And the night Daddy got better?" Martha asked.

"Everybody saw the star. Even the dogs bowed down, like they saw it, too."

And Martha knew what she had to do. She and Grandma had to figure out some way, no matter what it took, to get *everybody* out to *the* tree on Christmas Eve. *Even Scooter-Doo!*

"Jamie," Martha called as she went out into the hall. "Come on in and see Grandma."

Jamie skipped down towards Martha. "See you later, Bob," she called back to the old man, waving at him.

"Kids!" the old man sputtered, in spite of the grin on his face. "They don't have no respect at all. You'd think she could at least call me 'Gramps'."

Inside Grandma's room, Jamie went over to see Martha's grandma. She spoke softly and kindly to her. "It is good to see you again, Mrs. Ferguson."

Martha was standing behind Jamie. It was a good thing, because that way Jamie couldn't see her grin at Grandma when Grandma just sat, staring into space, like she didn't understand a word that was being said.

Good, Martha thought, *it's still our secret. I can't wait until Christmas Eve!*

CHAPTER EIGHT

Martha and Jamie were walking along the road when a voice called to them. "Hello, there!"

The girls turned to look, and Jamie gasped. There, right in front of them, stood...*Santa Claus!*

"You...you weren't kidding!" she whispered to Martha. "You really do know him."

"I told you," Martha said, heading for the old white-bearded figure. "Hi, buddy," she said, trying to sound familiar enough to impress Jamie.

"Hi, Martha," Santa said, causing Martha to grin widely at him.

Boy, she thought, *I'm sure glad he remembered my name.*

He paused for a few moments, trying to remember what Martha's friend's name was. Byron had told him Martha had gone to visit Bess with—*Janet, Janice, Janie, no it was Jamie...*To make an even deeper impression, he said as his memory came through for him, "You must be Martha's friend, Jamie."

"Wow!" Jamie said. "You're really good!"

"Of course I am," Santa said. "You didn't think Santa would be a bad boy, did you?"

"No," Jamie said. "I didn't mean..."

Santa laughed and rumpled her hair. "No harm done," he assured her. "Santa always knows what you mean, even before you say it."

Jamie wriggled around nervously. Did Santa really know if she'd been bad or good? Her mind raced over the last few weeks. She couldn't think of anything terrible she had done. She'd even been pretty kind to her brothers and sisters. And she had tried awfully hard to help Martha with all of her problems. Surely being a good friend of a friend of Santa's should count for something.

"Don't worry," Santa said, like he was a mind reader, "you're in the clear. I have seen only good things from your house. You'll get what you want for Christmas this year. Mark my words."

"Santa!" Martha said suddenly. Could he help them? They had just taken Grandpa's only Christmas tree away from him. His apartment wouldn't even look like Christmas without it. "Could you help me?" And she told him about them taking the little pinecone tree to her grandma.

"So you want a tree for your grandfather?" Santa asked.

Martha nodded. Soon they were headed for the nearest Christmas tree lot. Santa talked to the man who was running the lot. The next thing they knew, the three of them were dragging a good-sized Christmas tree over the snow-covered sidewalks.

"But Grandpa's apartment is over that way," Martha said, pointing in the opposite direction. "You know, where we were yesterday."

"I know," Santa said, his eyes twinkling and his cheeks glowing red from the cold. "But we have one stop to make first." He walked right over to the hardware store.

She had seen the hardware store so many times, but she never went inside. She didn't know why, but her dad always insisted that she wait for him out in the car. As she thought about it, she could not remember ever seeing any of her friends going inside. Martha had often wondered what was so secret about a plain old hardware store.

"You girls wait out here," he instructed. "I'll be back in just a minute." And he disappeared, leaving Martha to wonder just what was so secret inside the little hardware store.

When Santa returned, he carried two huge shopping bags filled with Christmas lights, ornaments of every sort, and four packages of tinsel.

Martha laughed when she saw the bags. "We're going to have to make a bunch of trips, aren't we?"

"Probably," Santa said, then asked, "Is your grandpa home?"

"I don't know," she replied.

"I hope not," Santa said. "Wouldn't it be fun if we could get the tree all trimmed before he came home?"

Jamie, now over the shock of walking down Main Street with Santa Claus, entered into the spirit of the moment. "Yes, and you're even tall enough to put the star on top."

Soon they were at Grandpa's apartment building. They struggled to get the tree inside the front door, then Santa went directly to the elevator and punched the button for "Up."

"Why don't you two wait here while I go see if he's home?" Martha suggested.

"Good idea," Santa said. "Maybe I should take you along with me on Christmas Eve. I could use a good helper."

Martha and Jamie both gasped. Was he serious? Imagine riding with Santa in his sleigh all around the world!

"No!" Martha said suddenly. "I'm really sorry, but I can't."

Jamie nudged Martha in the ribs with her elbow. "What's the matter with you? How can you pass on *that?*"

"I have something more important to do," Martha said, remembering the plan she had started to make with her grandmother. "I have to go to a very special Christmas tree."

"Oh, my!" Santa said, slapping his gloved hands against his round cheeks. "I almost forgot about *the* tree. How selfish of me! Of course that is more important."

"Is *the* tree really that important?" Jamie asked.

"Oh, yes," Santa said, winking at Martha. "It is a tree that is filled with miracles. *Christmas* miracles! The kind that only happen once a year. And I don't think Martha can afford to wait another whole year for the miracles she needs."

Martha ran ahead to the apartment door and quietly tiptoed inside. She looked all around, then came back and stuck her head out the door and waved Santa and Jamie inside. "The coast is clear," she said, bubbling over with the excitement of their little Christmas surprise for her grandfather.

* * *

Santa was just sticking the star on the top of the tree when the door opened and Grandpa came in.

"Whatever...?" Grandpa asked.

"Don't you ever knock?" Santa asked, adding a big *Ho! Ho! Ho!* "You could give a guy a heart attack."

"Not on my own door," Grandpa said, laughing. "I do, however, usually expect guests to wait until they are invited inside."

"I'm sorry, Grandpa," Martha said. "We wanted to surprise you."

"Well, you did that, all right," Grandpa said. He went over and put one arm around Martha and the other one around Jamie. "And I have to say, it was a pretty nice surprise." He studied the tree carefully. "It's the prettiest tree since...since your grandmother and I decorated *the* tree the last time."

"Grandpa," Martha asked, rolling her big round eyes at him, "Will you take me to *the* tree on Christmas Eve?"

"I've been thinking about that," Grandpa said. "I think we should all go to *the* tree this year. I think we could all use a miracle."

"You've got that right," Santa said, his face suddenly filling with sadness. It had been almost a year since his own wife had died, and it didn't seem like Christmas—not even to a Jewish Santa Claus. Yes, he could use a miracle, too, but he wasn't part of the family. He knew he wasn't invited. His mind began to whir. He wondered how he could manage to get himself invited. He'd have to work on that one.

Neither Grandpa nor Martha mentioned that Grandma had told them they should go to *the* tree. That would have to wait, Martha thought. If everything worked the way it should, Grandma could tell them all herself.

CHAPTER NINE

Joan sat in the recliner, wondering where Martha was. It was way past the time for her to have come home from school. *Please let her be at Dad's,* she prayed silently, but she could not summon the energy she needed to get up to phone him to find out.

She didn't know what was the matter with her; first, there was the ongoing argument between her and Max; second, there was Martha's disappearance, and she felt like that was all her fault; then there was the visit with Mom, with her insistence that she had to go to *the* tree on Christmas Eve.

Was something physically wrong with her, or was she losing her mind? Either way, she had to do something about it. She knew it wasn't fair to Martha for her to act the way she had been lately. It was almost Christmas, and she didn't want to ruin it for her daughter. Or for Max, either, she admitted. She had never been really crazy about children, but she loved her daughter. It was just that she had no experience with them at all, which made it hard for her to interact with them. When other girls had been babysitting, she had been busy with drama class and her ballet and her piano lessons.

Piano! It was sheer inspiration. She pulled herself up and went to the piano. The cover was closed; it had been far too long since she had touched the instrument. Once she had gotten such satisfaction out of her music, but she had forsaken it, and she didn't even know exactly when or why.

As she began to play, songs she had learned when she was just a child, she smiled—for the first time in a long time. "I can always tell how you feel by the way you play," her father always told her. He was right, she knew. If that was the case, the way she felt right now was scared, in need of protection, confused.

The door swung open and Max came in. He sat on the bench beside her, putting his arm around her and drawing her close to him.

"Is it that bad?" he asked.

For no reason at all, Joan began to sob uncontrollably. "I don't know what's the matter with me," she said when she could finally talk. She clung to him as though he were her lifeline. "Max, I think something is wrong with me. Maybe I caught it from your mother."

Max laughed. "We don't know what Mom has, or what triggered her loss of memory, but I am certain it isn't contagious."

"Maybe it's something in her genes," Joan said.

"And since when does a person get the genes of their in-laws?" Max asked.

"I'm not making any sense at all, am I?"

"Not a lot," Max said, continuing to hold her. He had sensed that there was something wrong, but he'd known better than to broach the subject with her. Finally, in her own time, she was ready to confide in him. He did love her, and he felt that love renewed with her vulnerability. "Why don't I set up an appointment with Phil for you? It's been quite a while since you've seen him."

"I didn't have any reason to see him," Joan said, "I'm not sick."

"You may not be sick, but something is not right. Maybe Phil can figure it out."

"But why can't you figure it out?" Joan asked. "You're a doctor—a good one!"

"You know we can't treat our own family members," Max said. "Besides, I'm probably a little too close to the situation to be completely objective." He put his hands on her face and turned it upwards towards him. He kissed her, gently, as though she might break if he applied too much pressure. "Have I told you lately that I love you?"

There was no reason for her outburst, but his confession of love sent her into howling hysterics again.

"Come on," he said, taking her hand and leading her up the stairs. "Why don't you lie down for awhile? Maybe if you get some rest…"

"Martha!" Joan said. "She isn't home yet."

"She's over with Dad," Max said. "He called to let me know." He wondered if he should tell her what Dad had said about calling the house and how he had let it ring and ring but no one had answered it. He decided not to pursue the matter, but wait until Phil Martin, one of his co-workers at the clinic, had a chance to examine her. *Oh, God, don't let anything be wrong with her,* his heart cried out. *Not now! It's Christmas time!*

Max helped his wife into bed, then reached over into his emergency medical bag that he always kept nearby. He took out a bottle, checked it, then handed her a tranquilizer. He wondered how long it had been since she had had a good night's sleep.

"What's this for?" she asked him.

"It will help you sleep."

"I don't need it," she insisted. "Just stay with me. *Please!*" Her voice sounded desperate.

"I'm right here," he said, sitting on the bed beside her, running his fingers over her hair and soothing her like she was a little girl. In less than five minutes she was sound asleep. He stayed with her until he heard the front door open. He went down to find his dad and Martha coming in.

"Dad," he said, "I think there's something wrong with Joan."

Byron nodded towards Martha, warning Max not to say too much in front of the child. Max caught the look and nodded, indicating that he understood.

"Why don't you go out in the kitchen and get a can of pop for Grandpa and me?" Max asked.

"Okay," Martha said, heading for the kitchen. As soon as she got through the door, she pushed it back open just a crack so she could hear them.

"I'm going to make an appointment for her to see Phil tomorrow," Max explained to his father. "I can tell there's something wrong."

Martha couldn't stop herself. She ran back into the living room and asked her father, "Daddy, is Mommy going to die?"

Max stared at his daughter. She looked back up at him, her body rigid with fear.

"No, honey," he said, trying to sound as reassuring as he could. "I'm sure it is nothing serious, but we need to have Dr. Phil take a look at her to find out what it is." He hesitated, then said, "I know you've noticed that she hasn't been herself lately."

"Then who is she?" Martha asked, sounding confused.

"I didn't mean that she is somebody else," Max explained. "I just meant that she hasn't been feeling good, so we need to find out why. That way Dr. Phil can fix her all up."

"But Daddy," Martha argued, "Mommy doesn't need a doctor! All she needs is to go to *the* tree. Grandma said so!"

Martha bit her lips and shivered. She had sworn to Grandma that she wouldn't tell anybody their secret. Now what had she done?

CHAPTER TEN

There were only two days left until Christmas Eve. Martha was anxious to see all her cousins, aunts and uncles, who would be arriving today. While Martha's father had chosen to stay in Hibbing to practice medicine, the other siblings from the family had scattered far and wide: Kathy was a nurse and lived in Chicago; Bill was a high school coach and taught history in Duluth, where he and his wife had three kids; and Carol and her husband had six children of their own and took in foster children besides. She didn't need to work; she had more than enough to do with what Max called "her brood." "Seventeen of them all together!" Grandpa had said the other day as he added them all up, joking because he had long ago run out of enough fingers. Max had made reservations at local motels for them, hoping it would help ease the strain on Joan.

Martha thought about the plan she and Grandma had been putting together. Now, there seemed to be only one problem left: how would they all get to *the* tree on Christmas Eve? Grandpa's jeep and her dad's pickup, even with the camper on the back, couldn't hold everybody. Martha knew she would have to go visit Grandma to see if she had a solution. She grinned, proud of knowing that she was the only one Grandma had confided in. Yes, somehow or other they would figure it out.

"Daddy!" she called out.

"Up here," he answered from upstairs. It made Martha nervous that her mother seemed to be so—she didn't even want to think the word—*sick*. It was Christmas; her mother had to be okay. If only she could get her to *the* tree, she knew everything would be all right. Grandma had promised.

"I'm going over to see Grandma," Martha said.

"You'd better wait and let me drive you," Daddy said. "It's thirty-six below zero. You'll freeze to death."

"I'll be okay, I promise," she insisted, but Daddy stood just as firm. Finally she gave in and agreed to let him take her.

"Call me when you are ready to come home," he said as he stopped at the front door of the nursing home.

Martha hesitated before she got out. "Is…is Mommy going to be all right?" she asked. A tear trickled down her cheek as she said, "I'm scared!"

"She went to see Dr. Phil yesterday," Daddy said. "I'm going to take her today to get the results of the tests."

"I hope it's good news," Martha said, sounding way too grown up for her six years. "I'll tell Grandma 'hi' from you."

"Give her a kiss and a hug, too," he said as she jumped out and ran up the sidewalk, trying to keep ahead of the cold.

* * *

Max's mind wandered as he drove back home to get Joan. They'd had their ups and downs over the years, like any other couple, but nothing like this. She had been apprehensive while carrying Martha, but as soon as she saw her, an instant bond formed between them. He had no idea she had harbored such feelings of guilt all these years. They'd been so happy when they were dating. What had gone wrong? Was it his fault?

He drove faster. The pickup fishtailed on the ice as he swerved to avoid another car. It snapped him back to the present, making him aware that he had better keep his mind on his driving. If nothing else, Martha needed him—now more than ever—with Joan acting so uptight about everything.

As he drove, he thought about life at home. He realized that with his medical practice being so demanding, he hadn't been as attentive to Joan's needs as he should have been. He vowed that as soon as they finished at Dr. Phil's, he would do everything in his power to remedy the situation.

He pulled the car into the driveway, jumped out with the motor still running so it wouldn't be cold for her, and ran into the house.

"Joan!" he hollered. "I'm here to take you to see Phil. Are you ready?"

There was no response, only the silence of an empty house. Scooter Doo was lying on the sofa, as she had done so much lately. She looked up at him, raising an eyebrow, then cowered back into the corner.

Max raced upstairs, afraid Joan was so sick that she wasn't able to get out of bed. Finding the bed empty, but unmade, he grabbed the phone and called the clinic.

"This is Dr. Max," he said to the receptionist. "Is my wife there?"

"She just left," the receptionist said.

"Did she see Dr. Phil?"

"Yes," came the reply.

"Put me through to him!" Max said, his voice demanding, not soothing and comforting.

"Dr. Phil speaking."

"Phil? It's me, Max."

"Hi, Max. What's up? I've seen two of your patients you had scheduled. Everything all right?"

"You tell me!" Max shouted at his fellow physician. "You saw Joan?"

"Yeah, she just left."

"What did you find out?" Max asked nervously, sitting down for the news, prepared for the worst and hoping for the best.

"I'm afraid I can't tell you," Phil said. "She made me promise that I would let her tell you."

"But I'm a doctor, too. You know you can tell me," Max protested.

"I'm sure she'll be there any minute. Don't worry; she's fine."

"Then why isn't she here?"

"Calm down, man," Phil said. "I told you, she's fine. It takes a while with the roads as icy as they are."

"Tell me about it!" Max snapped, recalling the near accident he had just a couple of blocks from home.

"Hey, man!" Phil said, again trying to calm him down. "Get a hold of yourself."

"Okay," Max said. "I'll be fine. Or at least I will be as soon as she gets home. 'Bye."

He slammed the receiver onto the cradle and started to pace, glancing at his watch every few seconds. The minutes seemed to loom into hours. *Where was she? Had she had an accident? Should he call the police to find out? Stop being so paranoid!*

The door slammed shut and he raced to see her. He wanted to hold her in his arms, like he hadn't done for way too long. He wanted to tell her that he loved her. He wanted to kiss her, to feel her hair, to make love to her…

* * *

Martha got a ride home with one of the nurses from the nursing home who lived near them. She hadn't bothered to call, as she often rode with the neighbor.

"Daddy!" Martha called out when she ran into the house. "Are you here? I got a ride with Nancy. And why is the car still running?"

Max had completely forgotten about the car. "I'll go shut it off," he said, walking out the door without putting his jacket back on. "I'll be right back in."

When he came back inside, Martha asked, "Where's Mommy?"

"She went to see Dr. Phil," he said.

"I thought you were going with her," Martha said. She looked at her father's face and saw the fear that was so evident. "Daddy! What's the matter with Mommy?"

"Nothing," Max said, trying to convince himself as much as his daughter. "Mommy wanted to do this on her own. But I talked to Dr. Phil and he said she is just fine."

"Are you sure?" Martha asked, going over and standing directly in front of him.

"Dr. Phil said so," Max insisted. "He would know if anything was wrong."

Martha seemed satisfied, at least for the moment. But a gnawing feeling inside Max's head and heart told him that he wasn't at all so sure of it. He remembered the day she had left. What if she did that again? *It was Christmas, for God's sake! Didn't she know what she was doing to them?*

The doorbell rang, and Max ran to get it. *Dear God, don't let it be the police!* he prayed silently, remembering countless TV scenes where tragic news had been heralded by a ringing doorbell.

"Merry Christmas!" Carol said as their entire brood tumbled into the house. "Jerry will be here in a couple of minutes. He's getting the presents."

Max breathed a sigh of relief when Martha immediately began entertaining her cousins and the foster cousins who always accompanied the family. At least for the moment, things seemed to be under control.

He looked at his watch again. It really wasn't time to start worrying yet.

Before Jerry got inside, two more cars pulled into the yard and people began tumbling inside. It was Kathy who finally asked, "Where's Joan?"

Max's face tensed. He didn't know what to tell them. He didn't want to lie, because if she didn't show up pretty soon they would know there was trouble in his marriage. But he would have to tell them something, and knowing his brother and sisters, it had better be convincing.

"She had to run over to the clinic," he said, hoping that would end it. He should have known that Kathy would pick up on that; he had never been able to put anything over on her.

"Forget something at work?" Bill asked, teasing his brother.

"No," Kathy said. "Something's wrong."

"Oh, you old worry wart," Bill said, nudging her playfully.

"No," Kathy said. "I'm sure of it." She paused, then said, pointing at Max, "Look at him. He's not...*normal!*"

They all laughed at that. "He's never been *normal,*" Carol said.

Max tried to deflect the attention away from himself. "Look who's talking; you with your dozen kids. Now *that's* not normal!"

"Quit changing the subject," Kathy said. "What's the matter with Joan?"

Max realized there was no point in trying to dodge the issue; he knew Kathy wouldn't let it rest until she knew the whole story. So, he began by telling them about her recent strange moods, and how they had argued about having more children, and about how she felt she really didn't even want—or love—Martha.

"That's awful!" Carol said. She couldn't imagine how empty her life would be if she was childless. "It's not normal."

Max was starting to hate that word. He wondered if there was such a thing as normal. And who decided what was normal and what wasn't.

"So when is she coming back from the clinic?" Bill asked.

"I..." Max was in tears. "I don't know *if* she's coming back."

"What do you mean?" Kathy demanded. "Why wouldn't she?" She shook her head as she realized what he might be saying. "You two aren't...*separated*...are you?"

"I don't think so," Max said. "She did leave one day, but the next day she came back." Again, he was sobbing. "It was just awful for Martha."

"Probably not too great for you, either," Bill said, putting his arm around his brother's shoulders.

They were interrupted by the sound of someone outside. Before Max could get to the door, the Ferguson Four's father pushed the door open and nearly collapsed as he got inside.

"Dad!" Max said, running to grab him before he fell. "What on earth is wrong?"

"It's Bess," he said, his voice hardly audible. "She's...*gone!*"

"What?" Max asked, his voice much too loud suddenly. "But I saw her just yesterday and she was fine. Well, as fine as she ever is. What happened? Was it a heart attack? There weren't any signs of trouble yesterday."

Max led Grandpa over to the big recliner, where he hurried to check his pulse.

"No," Grandpa said. "It isn't her heart. At least I don't think so. She's not *gone* gone. She's disappeared. They've looked all over and no one can find any sign of her."

"That doesn't make any sense," Kathy said. "I'm going over there, right now." She grabbed her hat and scarf and headed for the door. "I'll call as soon as I know anything."

"Maybe we should all go," Max said.

"No, you stay here in case Joan shows up," Kathy said, making perfect sense, as usual. "Besides, somebody has to keep an eye on Dad and the kids are all upstairs playing."

No one argued with her. When it came to common sense matters, nobody ever argued with Kathy. They all knew she was usually right.

* * *

"What have you done with my mother?" Kathy asked as she burst into the director's office.

"I haven't done anything with her," the director replied. "We have everyone looking. I'm sure she will show up soon."

"*Soon?*" Kathy shouted. "Soon isn't good enough. I want her found *now!*"

"I told you, we are doing everything we can to try to locate her," he said, sounding far too patronizing.

"Fine!" Kathy snapped. "I'll just go look for myself!"

She went up and down the corridors, going into her mother's room and checking in the closet and even under the bed. There was no sign of her mother anywhere. She went back to the closet and looked inside. It was odd, she thought, that there was no coat there. She hurried out into the hall and hailed a nurse.

"Do you know if my mother had a coat in her closet?" she asked.

"Of course," the nurse said. "I took her outside for some fresh air just this week. She had her black and white tweed jacket on." She paused, trying to picture it. "It had a hood on it, but she put a red wool scarf on her head instead."

Kathy went back to her room to check again, but there was no sign of either the jacket or the red scarf. She went back out into the hall and began to question everybody she met. Finally, one of the elderly man residents said, "She left a little while ago."

"Left?" Kathy asked.

"Yup," he said. "Dr. Max's wife, she came and got her. I didn't think nothin' of it. Just figured she was taking her home for Christmas."

"They left in a car?" Kathy asked, relieved that she was with Joan. Then she remembered what Max had said about Joan's state of mind, and the scenario went from bad to worse. Were there two members of the Ferguson family, wandering around in near 40 below zero weather, at least a little bit loony?

"Yup," the man said. "It was a dark red van-like thing."

Yes, Kathy thought, *that sounds like Joan's mini-van.* Max would know the license number; they could call the police and get them to put an APB.

Kathy went to the nurses' station and picked up the phone.

"Hey!" a large, gray-haired nurse chided. "You aren't allowed to use that phone. That's for personnel only."

"Watch me!" Kathy said as she dialed 911.

"We have a missing person," she said into the phone.

"Less than an hour," she said.

"What do you mean, you have to wait twenty-four hours? This is a sick old lady and her wacky daughter-in law! Now, get out there and find them!"

She hesitated, listening, then snapped into the phone, "Fine! I'll go find them myself! Thanks a lot!" She slammed the phone down so hard it was a wonder it didn't crack in two.

* * *

"Joan picked her up," Kathy said as she walked into Max's house. "Did they show up?"

"No," Max said, still obviously shaken. "What do we do now?"

Martha and all of her cousins came into the room just in time to hear the conversation.

"Mommy picked *who* up?" Martha asked.

"Grandma," Max said, picking Martha up in his arms and holding her so tight she almost couldn't breathe. "We think maybe she was going to surprise us by bringing her home for Christmas."

"No," Martha said firmly. "They aren't coming home."

They all stared at Martha. "What do you mean?" Max asked.

"They went to *the* tree," Martha said, as if that would explain everything.

"Mommy and Grandma went to *the* tree?" Max asked, obviously puzzled.

"Yes," Martha said. "Grandma told me that we all had to go to *the* tree on Christmas Eve."

Suddenly both Max and Grandpa said at the same time, "She told me that, too."

"Mom talked?" Carol asked. "Why didn't you tell us?"

"I didn't think much about it," Max said. "That was all she said. Just '*Go to the tree.*'"

Martha wiggled in her daddy's arms. She wondered if she should still guard the rest of their secret. What if they *didn't* go to *the* tree? What if they never found her mommy or her grandma? It would all be her fault.

As if to avoid any problems, Max said, "We have to go to *the* tree. It has to be where they have gone."

"But how will we all get there?" Bill asked. "Our two little cars will never make it to Sawbill Landing with all the snow."

"I'll call Geo…*Santa Claus,*" Grandpa volunteered. "He's got that big old bus he rigged to take supplies out to the camp. That thing could make it through anything. Besides, he's got a plow hooked up on the front of it."

Martha looked confused. "But Daddy, it's almost Christmas Eve! Santa Claus can't go with us! He has to deliver all the toys."

"Some things are more important than toys," Max said, trying to explain what he couldn't understand himself. "Family and the people we love, that is what Christmas is all about. God sent His Son, the baby Jesus, to earth because He loved all of us. That's what Christmas is all about; it's all about love."

Grandpa was on the phone, talking too softly for them to hear what he said. In a few minutes he turned to them and said, "He will be here in about ten minutes, as soon as he fills it up with gas. He said he would love to go out there with us. He says he's heard about *the* tree, and has always wanted to visit it—especially on Christmas Eve—but he was always too busy."

"But what about all the kids and what they want for Christmas?" Martha asked.

"He said his brother has been begging for a chance for years to take his route on Christmas Eve. Guess this is his big break."

"Wow! Are we in luck or what?" Bill said, trying to lighten the mood. "Come on, everybody, get bundled up. When we get out to the old house, it will be cold. We'll have to get a fire going right away."

* * *

There wasn't much conversation on the ride out to Sawbill Landing. Everybody's mind was on Joan and Grandma. They had to find them, and they had to be all right. It was Christmas, and nothing could happen to either of them. They all loved them far too much for anything to go wrong.

CHAPTER ELEVEN

As Grandpa's jeep, Max's van, and Santa's bus turned onto the road that led to Grandpa's house at Sawbill Landing, everyone could see the smoke pouring out of the chimney. They all breathed a sigh of relief when they saw Joan's van parked in front of the house. As soon as the three vehicles stopped, everyone piled out. There was no denying it; there was something magical and mysterious just by being here. Even Scooter Doo walked off the bus on her own power.

Martha had pleaded with her father to take her along to *the* tree. "Scooter Doo needs a miracle, too." Max had to agree with her on that. She really hadn't been herself for several months, and the last few weeks had gotten harder for her. Yes, Scooter Doo, like the rest of the family, needed her own miracle.

Grandpa ran into the house well ahead of the rest of them.

"Bess!" he called out. "Bess! Where are you? Bess!" There was no response.

Grandpa ran through the house, calling her name as he went. Still, there was no reply.

"Grandpa," Martha said, tugging on his jacket. "They are already at *the* tree."

"How do you know?" he asked.

"Look there!" Martha said, pointing to the tracks from their forsaken snowmobile. They led directly into the woods, right towards *the* tree. Soon they were all running, as fast as they could, towards the highest tree in the forest.

Grandpa stopped along the way to catch his breath, his mind playing over all the stories he had heard about the miracles that had happened to family members since the first time his grandmother and Hjelmer Finseth had decorated it. It had been trimmed every year after that, until the camp had closed. It remained alone, waiting for someone to return so it could fulfill its purpose in life, even if it was for one last time.

"There it is!" Max announced, his voice filled with pride and admiration at being the first to spot it.

They hurried to the tree. As they gathered in front of it, they stared up at the huge pine. It seemed to shine, even without any Christmas lights. It was, much to their surprise, already decorated. There were pinecones and red berries, bird nests and a squirrel chattering in its branches. It was, they could see, nature's trimming. Then, to their utter astonishment, Grandma poked her head out from among the branches several feet up from the ground.

"Bess!" Grandpa shouted. "Come down from there right this minute!"

With even greater surprise to all of them, *Grandma answered back!* "We aren't done yet." She dangled an "angel's hair" she had formed from the silk inside some milkweed pods. "It isn't finished until we get this hung up."

"It's a miracle!" Max said, his voice filled with awe. "Grandma is talking!"

Martha looked up at Grandma, who winked at her. They would never tell anyone that she had been talking for some time. No, that was their little secret. If they wanted to believe it was a miracle, what was wrong with that?

"Mom!" Max called up to her. "Where is Joan? Is she all right?"

"I'm right here," Joan said as she jumped down from a lower branch. She went over to Max, stretched up on her tiptoes and kissed him. Not a reluctant, "have-to" kiss, but a warm, tender "I-love-you" kiss. "I have a surprise for you," she said.

"You scared me half to death!" Max scolded her. "Why didn't you at least call me after you saw Phil to let me know what he said? You could have told me you were coming out here."

Joan put her finger over his mouth in an attempt to shush him.

"Do you want to know what the surprise is?" she asked him. "It is Christmas, you know."

"Of course I want to know, now that I know you're all right. Okay, little lady, what's your great surprise?"

She pulled his hood until his head was low enough that she could whisper in his ear.

"You're sure?" Max asked. When she nodded, he yelled at the top of his lungs into the forest for all of the family—and nature itself—to hear: "We are going to have a baby!"

A round of applause went up on all sides of them.

"Dr. Phil said the only thing wrong with me was hormones," Joan said, laughing. "That and the fact that he thinks I am carrying three babies inside me. He'll know for sure when he does an ultra sound in a few weeks."

"*Three?*" Max asked, his eyes round with shock.

"Guess you'll just have to learn to put up with me until I deliver them."

"You mean I'm going to have three brothers or sisters?" Martha asked. "All at once?"

"That's right," Joan said, hugging her daughter tightly. "Triplets. And I can only hope that they are half as good as you are." She kissed her daughter tenderly. "I love you, Martha Ferguson."

"Look!" Max said, pointing way up on the tree. "It's Hjelmer's angel." There, nestled in the branches was the wooden angel he had carved for Maya that Christmas so long ago at Sawbill Landing.

"They were my grandparents," Grandma said as she climbed down from the tree into Grandpa's arms. "He was so tall…"

"How tall was he?" the children all asked together.

"He was so tall that he didn't even need a ladder to put it up there."

They all laughed together. Suddenly, there was a high-pitched whine from behind *the* tree. Bill went back to investigate. He came back, motioning for them to follow him, but to be quiet. There, nestled in a little pile of pine branches, was Scooter Doo—and three brand new tiny puppies.

"It's a miracle!" Martha exclaimed. "Three of them. Just like Mommy's going to have!"

Grandpa looked heavenward, offering a prayer of thanks. Thanks for Bess. Thanks for his entire family. Thanks for one more year of miracles.

"Come here!" he said anxiously. "Stand right here by me."

They all congregated as close to him as they could get. "Up there," he said.

There was one tremendous gasp as they all saw it; the star was in the perfect position so it topped *the* tree, just like it had done every other year when true miracles happened.

* * *

Grandma sat on the sofa at Max's house on Christmas day. The other women were washing the dishes, the men were watching TV, and the children were all busy with their new toys. *Santa* sat there beside her.

"It was quite a Christmas, wasn't it?" Santa—alias George—remarked.

"Yes, even for one Jewish hardware store owner," she said, winking playfully at him.

They sat silently for a while, contemplating the events of the last few days. Bess finally spoke. "You know, every one of the miracles that happened could have occurred just as easily without *the* tree. Sometimes I think we are all responsible for making the miracles happen that we need."

"You might be right," Santa said. "But it never hurts to have a little help along the way."

"You better watch out, or you might even start believing in Christmas," Bess said, chuckling.

"Who says I don't believe?" Santa asked. He didn't see Martha peeking around the corner as he said, "Santa *has to* believe in Christmas, or at least the meaning of Christmas. If he didn't, it wouldn't be Christmas." Then he leaned over and kissed Bess on the cheek. They had been friends for so many years, and it was really good to have her back again. He missed his own wife so much, but at least he had his old friend back.

Martha climbed back up the steps to join her cousins, singing as she went, "I saw Grandma kissing Santa Claus…"

A NOTE FROM THE AUTHOR

Our great country of America is filled with memories of things that were: things that mattered, things that were typical of a bygone era, things that are no more. Logging camps deep in the middle of forests are one of those memories. Stories of Paul Bunyan and his blue ox, Babe, make it seem like a bigger-than-life part of our history. Sawbill Landing was one of those logging camps. There was not a Paul Bunyan. There was not even a Hjelmer Finseth. But to me, it was a very real place. I spent two very special weeks there one summer, many years ago, when I was teaching Vacation Bible School for the American Sunday School Union. A figment of my imagination became a part of my reality.

To this end, I vowed long ago that one day I would honor the men and women who sacrificed so much every day so the rest of the country could have the things we deemed a necessity, but which they considered a luxury.

Sawbill Landing was, as in the book, not too far from Hibbing, Minnesota. My previous Christmas book, *A Christmas Dream,* like *A Lumberjack Christmas...Revisited* is set on the Iron Range of Minnesota (Duluth, MN).

For all of you, I truly wish you all the warmth and joy of Christmas. But most of all, I wish you your very own Christmas miracle. That is, after all, what Christmas is all about. A miracle when God became Man, and a tiny Babe was sent to redeem the whole world. Can there be a greater miracle than that?

Merry Christmas to all, and to all a good night.

Janet Elaine Smith

Janetelainesmith@yahoo.com

See more about me and my other books at www.janetelainesmith.com (As always, I love to hear from readers.)

Printed in the United States
39097LVS00003B/253